A Farewell To Magic

Damian Woods

Copyright © 2024 Damian Woods

All rights reserved.

ISBN: 9798333801906

DEDICATION

I dedicate this book to all those lovers of fantasy the world over. Epic or personal, silly or serious, it has the power to transport us to brand new worlds.

CONTENTS

Acknowledgments   i

Prologue   1

Part One   7

Part Two   72

Epilogue   149

Afterword   158

ACKNOWLEDGMENTS

I would like to acknowledge all the authors and filmmakers both past and present who have dedicated their lives to creating amazing worlds and fantastical creatures that have made my imagination soar.

PROLOGUE

The vastness of the infinite. Stars, planets, comets. All the colours in existence, floating through space, glowing, shining, bursting... a firework display for the universe. Endless possibilities play out here. Tendrils of time and existence spread like tree roots in all directions.

This is the stage.

The curtains are opening.

Now, where to begin?

A long time ago, in a galaxy far…

No, not that.

Space! The final fron…

No, not that either.

Though it does have to do with space. And galaxies.

There are rather a lot of galaxies in this universe of ours (look it up), and so it stands to reason that there are planets within those galaxies that are 'Earth-like'. Or 'Earth-*ish*', if you prefer. Maybe they don't exactly mirror Earth as *we* know it, but it is safe to assume that there are similarities.

There is one particular 'Earth', in one particular galaxy, that is the focus of this story. So, it *is* in a galaxy far away. And it happened a long time ago, too.

The planet is known as Ethera. It's one defining difference, is magic.

On this planet, magic exists.

Magic is the very foundation of the life upon it. It's has got all the usual stuff, of course- trees, plants, banana's, horses, monkeys, income tax, etc, but it also has trolls and dragons, enchanted forests and… wizards. When the world was first created, its 'maker', known by philosophers, religious leaders and general church-bothering folk as The Great One, sent down ten wizards, and it was the job of the ten, to manage the whole creative process – to shape the mountains and the forests, to order the animals so they all didn't look too alike, or indeed, too weird (doesn't explain the duck-billed platypus though, does it?).

And it was also their job to supervise the creation of humanity, and ready them for the eventual running of the planet.

At that point, the magic would fade, and the job of the wizards would be over. No one was 100% sure what would happen then; if the wizards would fade away or fly off into the heavens to join The Great One, or just bugger off to a quiet corner and put their feet up.

No one was sure, because it didn't all go as planned.

The name of The Great One was never uttered. Most god-fearing folk were under the impression that the name of The Great One was just too holy to ever be spoken. Everyone else thought the religious leaders didn't even know what his (they always said 'he') name even was. Or if they did, it was just too unbelievably stupid to write down – like 'Picklenicker', or 'Jeff'. And how important was this Great One anyway? If there were that many galaxies and that many planets, was there a Great One for each galaxy? Or one who just does it all? Do they time-share? Is there a rota?

But I digress.

When humanity had been firmly established and were busying themselves putting up castles, building villages, debating the merits of scatter-cushions and having the odd war, the wizards knew it was time to give up their magic and go.

But there were some who just didn't fancy it.

They liked it on Ethera, they liked having magic, and power, and didn't want to go anywhere. The other, more well-behaved wizards disagreed.

And so began the War.

That's right, it was so big and nasty, it needed a capital letter.

Now any war is bad enough, but a magical war could change the face of the world. As indeed it did. Oceans boiled, mountains fell, and all humanity could do was hold on tight and hope for the best.

There were humans who agreed with both outlooks, and even joined in the fighting. Kings and lords sending their armies forth like chess pieces in the ultimate game.

Legend has it, that it came down to two wizards – Rhyfeth and Hydeen. The duel took place in the Tower of Magic, set on an island of rock in the Silver Sea. The duel shook the very ground. The sea bubbled and steamed until it was no more. The tower cracked and split, and the magic could be seen lighting up the sky from miles and miles away.

When it was over, the Silver Sea had gone, and in its place was a wasteland of sand and rock. The Tower of Magic still stood but it was damaged beyond repair.

The wizards were never seen again.

That whole area became known as the Forbidden Lands. *Properly* forbidden, not in a 'oh alright then, the kids are at my mothers' kind of forbidden. The rest of the landscape, though shaken and damaged, was rebuilt by humanity and dubbed the Land of Ailani.

And as for the magic?

After the duel was over, the magic was gone.

PART ONE

1

The Forbidden Lands

The sand whipped and swirled viciously all around. There was so much of it in the air, the light of the sun could barely break through.

Kalem Huwaeth felt like he had been traveling through this sandstorm for weeks on end, when in reality, it had only been three days. But that was more than enough. Kalem, like the three other men with him, were wrapped up as tightly as possible, with barely a scrap of skin showing, not that it made much difference. The sand still got everywhere.

Everywhere.

He could feel it now between his butt-cheeks, rubbing up and down, *up and down*, with each undulation of the horse upon which he was riding. He started to think that eventually, his trousers would catch fire and any stray fart would rocket him into the atmosphere.

The force of the storm had made speedy travel impossible, so they had to move at an interminable crawl. Trying to find shelter was difficult, but not impossible. All around there were giant rocky outcroppings, some of which had enough over-hang to provide some protection, especially at night, so they could get a little sleep.

None of them grumbled out loud, at least not in intelligible words. He was sure, at times, he could hear strings of muffled expletives coming from beneath the folds of material that protected his men's faces. They wouldn't dare say too much, though. This was a very important mission after all. They were here searching for something.

Something precious.

And if they didn't bring it back, Kalem would not be happy. He had left his castle behind, guarded by his most trustworthy men, but still, every second away was agony. He had no aftershave and hadn't had a bath for days. Only the importance of the mission kept him going.

They would have to stop soon to take a break. Kalem kept his eyes peeled for a decent rocky shelter. *Hard to believe*, he thought, *that this was all ocean once.*

Indeed, it had been. A long, long time ago. Before the Council of Wizards had got it into themselves to have a little disagreement.

The home of the Council – that is, the Tower of Magic, had been in the midst of the ocean on a great island. Theoretically, it was still there. Kalem hoped so, because that is why they were here.

A large rock formation loomed out of the sandy murk. It looked like the giant crooked finger of a huge, unhappy monster trying to claw its way out of the ground. Shouting over the sound of the storm was useless, so Kalem used hand signals to point his men in the right direction. They moved over to the rock formation as one, slow organism, eager to escape into some kind of protection.

...

The men dismounted, pulling their horses under the protective rock as well as they could. The horses themselves were tired, their bits foamy. They hadn't come across any water for almost two days. Kalem – and his men – knew the poor beasts wouldn't last much longer.

The wicked whips of sand had lessened in the shade, so they pulled down the cloths that protected their faces to partake of their own meagre rations.
Kalem felt a moment of pleasure at being able to scrape away the sweaty cloth from his face. He was a handsome man, with a finely trimmed goatee beard and long, extremely well-kept black hair. It was a shame he had to keep it all bundled up inside his headgear. If it wasn't for the sand, he would let it all loose to flow heroically in the wind, as if he was advertising shampoo. But right now, he could sense the unease.

"It won't be much longer," he said, encouragingly.

The men didn't answer, just gave brief nods.

They rested for an hour, then Kalem gave the signal to move on. With bones creaking like un-oiled doors, they replaced the cloths on their faces and climbed back onto their horses.

The journey continued.

But not for long.

After only another ten minutes or so of slow progress, Kalem noticed something new. It wasn't rock. It wasn't sand. It was wood. A wooden pillar to be exact. To be even more exact, many of them. Kalem tried to relay his excitement to the men through frantic hand signals.

At first, they thought he had swallowed a bug. Eventually, they followed to where he was pointing and saw the uniform shapes sticking out of the ground. Moving toward them, they saw it was the wrecked remains of some kind of pier.

Of course! Thought Kalem. *The Tower of Magic would have had a pier for the boats that travelled to and from that sacred place.* He followed the wooden protrusions until they hit a massive mound of rock. Looking upward, Kalem and his men saw the great Tower of Magic looming over them, its hazy outline backlit by the scorching sun.

As they drew nearer, amazingly, the sandstorm lessened, and patches of blue sky appeared above them. Even the roaring of the sandstorm abated. "Lord!" called one of the men, excitedly. "Look!"

He was pointing to a large puddle of water, at least six feet across, that was being fed by a steady trickle of the precious liquid that seemed to come straight from the base of the tower itself.

Kalem dismounted.

He approached the puddle. The water looked clear and fresh. He took off one of his leather gloves and plunged his hand into it. It was refreshingly cold. Cupping some water in his hand he lifted it warily to his lips.

Was it safe? Was it poisonous? Was it salt water? He could have asked one of the men to taste it, he supposed, but after all these awful days of travel they would have drowned him in it.

He drank.

It was beautiful. Beautiful, cool, fresh water.
Kalem ordered them all to fill their skins, while he filled his. After that, he made sure the horses drank their fill.

Then he looked toward the tower.

2

The climb up over the rocky island toward the tower was not as bad as he feared it might be. Years and years of sandstorms had chipped away at the rock, creating useful hand and footholds.

They had tied the horses up safely below – in a shady spot away from the cruel sand – though admittedly it was far less of a problem in the vicinity of the tower. And he had kept the animals near the water.

The men had become noticeably more jovial since finding the structure – like the journey they had been on finally had a purpose, though the sight of the ominous building kept joking to a minimum. Who knows what was inside? Bodies? Treasure? Or maybe... nothing at all?

The ground level of the tower was covered in triangular stone paving slabs, the wind making the sand slide and dance across them. Kalem approached the large wooden doors of the building, signalling his men to follow. They all noticed, as they got closer, how damaged the great tower was. There were giant cracks in the stonework, great, gaping holes here and there, and scorch marks. *Evidence of a great magical battle.*

He tensed his muscles and prepared to push hard against the huge doors. At first, they wouldn't budge. He called his men to help him. They all put their shoulders to the ancient doors and shoved. It yielded only a little. They shoved again *and again* until finally the door yawned open, making a sound like a giant's burp. They entered.

The interior of the tower was a hexagonal shape, with a long winding staircase stretching up, and up, and *up*. Sand swirled about them even in here – invited in by the gaping holes that had penetrated the old stone. It had formed small dunes against the far walls.

There were beautiful murals painted upon the walls, depicting blue seas and green hills, vast mountains and pale skies, all faded now. Cracked and rotting. There were scorch marks, too. Black and charred indentations in the solid stone.

It must have been a hell of a battle, all right.
They started on their way up the stairs.

It was at this point Kalem began to worry. Just a little. He knew what he *wanted* to find. He knew what he *had* to find. He just wasn't totally sure it existed.

A thingy.

Now, most fantastical tales usually have a 'thingy' in them – could be a magical weapon, or a piece of jewellery, or a wand, or a staff.

But there is almost always a thingy.

Kalem was ardently hoping that he would find some such thingy in the tower, or something that would point the way to the thingy that he would need to accomplish his goals. He never believed that the magic had just vanished or faded. It had to *be* somewhere. *In* something. Hence… the thingy.

There were a few hairy moments on the way up the tower steps. Huge holes in the stone that let in a strong wind that curled around the interior of the tower, threatening to sweep the men either outward, or off the safety of the stairs and leave them plummet onto the ground below. In the end, they had to crawl past the holes on all fours, gripping at the steps with hands and feet like monkeys.

After many, many precarious minutes, Kalem and his men reached the top of the stairs. There was a single, large door, sapphire blue, set into the wall. He didn't know why, but Kalem drew his sword. The others followed suit. Taking a deep breath, Kalem approached the door. He reached out slowly, gripping one of the ornate gold doorhandles, and with another deep breath, he opened it.

They were indeed at the top of the tower. The Council-Room was lined with windows, so that the occupants could have looked out in any direction. Massive chunks of wall and roof were missing – destroyed, the jagged outlines charred black. Amazingly, patches of blue sky appeared through the hole in the roof. All about them, sand was heaped up in mounds on the floor, or lying lazily against the walls. In the middle of the great room was a vast oak table, hexagonal in shape. There were two shapes seated at it, though their forms were slumped and odd-looking.

Kalem and his men crept closer.

He could see plainly now, the shapes were skeletons, dressed ornately in coloured robes of silk. There were still spindly strands of grey hair clinging to their heads.

Well, to ONE of their heads. The other one didn't have a head.

They were sat at opposite ends of the table, reaching out toward what looked like an intricately carved staff, which lay in its centre.

Kalem's heart leapt. He dashed forward without thinking and picked up the object.

It was a thingy, all right. Or at least part of a thingy. Or a thingy holder. Looking at what he assumed was the top of the staff, there was a space for something to sit. Maybe an orb of some kind. Or a large crystal.

Suddenly, there was an unpleasant cricking, or cracking sound. Kalem froze. They all did. The noise, though quiet, had the illusion of great volume in this room. Kalem's eyes darted about, trying to

find the source. What could it have been? He looked at the skeleton. The one with the head.
It was looking right back at him.

"That doesn't belong to you" it said.

One of his men fainted, the others dropped their swords. Kalem, trying to look and act like a level-headed leader, twitched, though the scream that so desperately wanted to be let loose from his lips did a five-mile run around his brain cavity.
Instead of a scream, he managed to ask a question.

"Who are you?"

If the skeleton could have raised its eyebrows, it would have. "Who are you?" it asked back.

"Muh... my name is Lord Kalem Huwaeth of Nightstone Castle."

The empty skull seemed to mull on this a while. "I am Rhyfeth," it said, finally.

So, thought Kalem. *The legend was true.* It HAD come down to the two wizards. And Rhyfeth was the... winner? It had to be, seeing as he had a head, and Hydeen didn't. Legend had also written that Rhyfeth was the one who wanted to keep the magic and continue the dominion of wizards.

"What do you want?" asked the bony face.

Kalem was a little lost for words. He had not expected to have a conversation quite like this when he woke this morning.

"Come on," said Rhyfeth, impatiently. "I haven't got all day."

Gathering himself, Kalem responded.

"I seek to use the magic to destroy the Kingdom of Thayorn and rule over the land of Ailani myself."

If the skeleton of Rhyfeth could have stroked its chin, it would have. "And what then?" it asked. "Would you lock the magic away, never to be used again? Do you even know how to use it, human?"

This last question surprised Kalem a bit, as he realised, he hadn't even thought about it. He had assumed, along with the thingy, there might be a set of thingy instructions.
"I wouldn't lock the magic away," he answered. "It belongs in this world and should be part of it."

"But you still think a human should be in charge?"

This question from Rhyfeth came with what sounded like a smile. He was testing Kalem, and Kalem knew it.

"I think no one could ever truly rule well without magic. And..." he added hurriedly, "without a wizard by his side."

Rhyfeth made a strange sound, much like a handful of twigs being crushed in a plastic bag. Kalem realised it was a laugh.

"A good answer, human."

"May I ask," began Kalem, cautiously, "how you came to be, um, alive?"

The skeleton seemed to shrug. "During the final battle," he began, "there was magic all over the place. Raw, uncontrolled. Savage. Hydeen had created the staff you see there, and an orb, specially made, to hold the magic within it. You see, magic cannot be destroyed in the strictest sense of the word, but it can be contained. He had almost done it. I was losing, and I knew it. I used everything I had in those last moments to do two things. I cast a holding spell on myself, to keep my spirit here, within this form."

"And what was the second thing?" asked Kalem.

"I popped Hydeen's head off."

The skeleton emitted another twiggy chuckle. "He was dead, I was dying. I tried to reach out and take the staff, but it was all too much. The battle had done for me. I died here, my goal just out of reach. It was a real bummer."

"But where is the orb? Surely the staff is no good without it?"

"You are right there. After it was all over, King Thalra came to the tower. He had sided with Hydeen. I have a funny feeling Hydeen had spoken with him. Maybe gave him a few instructions on what to do if it all happened this way."

"What makes you think that?" asked Kalem.

"Because the cheeky bugger separated the orb from the staff and took it away, making the staff useless."

A thousand fireworks seemed to go off in Kalem's head. So, the orb MUST be in the Kingdom of Thayorn still, with the descendant of King Thalra.

"What if I took you with me?" declared Kalem. "I will take you and the staff back to my castle, and from there we will plot how to retrieve the orb."

Rhyfeth immediately agreed. After all, he'd been cooped up inside this tower for a considerable length of time now. More than two hundred years. He'd already named the bricks.

"The only problem is..." began Kalem, apologetically, "I don't think we can take *all* of you."

...

They left the tower with a spring in their step, knowing not only that they had found what they were looking for, more or less, but that they were now on their way back home, back to open air, and sand-free crevices. Kalem had given the staff to one of his men to carry, while he carried something else wrapped up in a cloth that dangled at his side. It was about the size of, well, a head.

"Hnow hong whill it thake hoo ghet therr?" came a voice from the folds of cloth.

Kalem opened the package and looked down at the grinning face within.

"What?"

"I said," repeated Rhyfeth, "how long will it take to get there?"

"It took us three days of travel to make it here. I plan to be back at Nightstone a lot quicker than that."

He closed the cloth bag and tied it securely to his horse. The small group mounted up and began the journey back home, all of them endeavouring to get out of the Forbidden Lands a lot quicker than they got into them. As they trotted away, back into the embrace of the sandstorm, all of them failed to notice the trickling water, that had made the life-saving pool.

It had stopped.

3

The Kingdom of Thayorn

The Kingdom of Thayorn is a rather... fancy place.

Lots of spires and fluttering flags, pale grey (and incredibly clean) stonework topped with dark red slate. Within the kingdom's walls, which surrounded the entire place, were many homes, and stalls, and businesses, while outside the walls, dotted about the lush green landscape, were farms and fields teeming with livestock of all kinds. Thayorn, basically, was full of life and boundless energy. There was one main gate that allowed people access into and out of the great kingdom, and this was only closed in times of war or danger, after as many innocent people as possible were brought within the safety of its walls.

Right now, Thayorn was in a state of excitement. The princess Evelynn had reached the age of fourteen, and the laws of the land stated she had now, legally, reached the age in which she could officially take over rulership of the entire kingdom, should anything happen to her parents, the king and queen. Known as First Rule Day. It was a pretty big deal, for a lot of reasons. It showed the royal parents that their daughter had reached an age of responsibility. It also showed trust in her and her abilities as a ruler.

There was a bit of nervousness as well, of course.

One can't help but pay attention to the niggling thought at the back of your mind that your offspring might have a streak of insanity in there that may lead them to think that the time to rule should come a lot sooner. Perhaps the rail around the balcony could be a bit loose, or some carless idiot might leave lots of sharp objects about the place that you could lose a limb on. But these thoughts were quickly batted away. Evelynn was a good, sweet, smart girl.

King Rolannd could see Evelynn now. He was stood on the balcony (he'd already checked the railing) of the tallest tower of the castle, looking down at her, moving through the crowds of people. She was well liked amongst the inhabitants of Thayorn. She smiled and talked and laughed with them, spent time with them, took an interest in them. Her father could see already that she would make an excellent queen. Just, not *too* soon, ay?

Queen Jocelyn joined her husband on the balcony, looking down at their daughter with pride. They enjoyed each-others smiles. Rolannd saw a lot of

Evelynn in her mother. Soft, corn coloured hair, beautiful green eyes. And she was smart too, smarter than he ever was, especially at that age.

"She is growing so fast, Rolannd."

He nodded and smiled, sadly. "Too fast."

There was a pause, the kind of pause that was hard to fill, though someone had to do it eventually.

"How are the preparations coming?" he asked, finally.

Rolannd, who may not be endowed with the greatest intellect in the world, did at least have a great deal of common sense when it came to organising celebrations. He got his wife to do it.

Jocelyn's eyes immediately lit up with excitement. "The banners are almost finished. As are the table decorations. Evelynn's gown was finished this morning. She looks beautiful, Rolannd."

The king smiled again. "I imagine she does."

"And what of your side of things?"

"I spoke with Captain Greeve yesterday. He has sent one of his best men to Flame Peak to speak to Hargan. And he assures me all the men will look resplendent on the day."

"I expect nothing less."

Rolannd suddenly got a bit edgy. "I've also, uh, sent out and invitation to... um...well, you know..."

Jocelyn's face dropped. "Oh, not him, Rolannd."

"I know, I know. But I can't very well leave him out, can I? He's family."

Jocelyn's lips twisted undefinably before she walked back into the castle. Rolannd just sighed.

...

Below, wandering happily through the crowds and market stalls, Evelynn smiled and waved at the people she knew, spoke to stall holders by name, returned polite nods to everyone who bowed and curtsied. She didn't mind being a princess. In fact, she rather enjoyed parts of it. She liked talking to people and helping to organise things. Making decisions was amongst her favourite activities. What she wasn't as fond of was all the parading around in fancy gowns with bits of precious metal stuck on her head. She understood that royal etiquette was important, and projecting a good image was necessary, *but my Great One*, it was booooring.

She much preferred being out amongst the people.

In fact, she decided that, when she became queen proper, it would be one of her main acts to tone down all the la-de-da and be a bit more, well, real.

She turned around and looked up at the castle, its impressive bulk managing to ooze a sense of royalty. It was her birthright. Her future. She wanted to do a good job, but she also didn't want to be shackled. She was lucky her parents weren't the smothering kind. Part of her job, she guessed, would be finding the balance. And speaking of that, she had to say a swift goodbye to the people around her and be on her way.

She had an appointment to get too.

...

There was a small, poky room in the castle, every corner of which was filled with thick, dusty books, every shelf on every wall filled with interesting little models and artefacts, and every spare chunk of wall had on it some old scroll or tapestry, depicting some historical event in the history of Ailani, or the kingdom of Thayorn. There was barely enough room for the small, wooden desk (covered in books and papers), two or three chairs (it was difficult to tell if there were two or three, as they were also covered in interesting bric-a-brac).

In amongst all this academical clutter was the equally academical Rhowern, a philosopher, adviser to the king, tutor, and just general know-it-all. He was pleasant enough, short, stubby, with a great big bushy beard that was so long, its end rested on top of his perfectly round pot belly. He was always humming to himself – a not unpleasant sound, though there was no recognisable tune in it. At this moment, he was rummaging around in a pile of some old, crinkly paper, looking for something or other.

The problem, he thought, w*ith knowing most things, especially about history, is that there is just so much of it, that some bits just plop out of your head after a while, so you always need a refresher.*

He was looking for information about the mating habits of trolls, for no other reason than he used to know it and didn't seem too anymore. It wasn't exactly good ice-breaking material, but it's the kind of thing that could randomly come up in the next pub quiz.

There was a knock at the door, and mere seconds later, it creaked open and Evelynn's smiling face appeared, along with the rest of her. For a moment, she couldn't see Rhowern anywhere, he was so hidden by the mountain of clutter.

"Rhowern?" she called. "Are you here?"

Suddenly, she heard a faint, semi-musical humming, and Rhowern appeared from behind a pillar of books. He saw her and smiled immediately.
"Ah! Princess Evelynn, my dear, please come in and take a seat."

She closed the door behind her and stepped into the room. The air, as usual, had a musty aroma, but it was a smell she had been used to since her infancy, learning letters and numbers and histories with Rhowern when his beard was much darker and his robe looser.

She approached one of the more visible chairs and absent-mindedly removed the books and papers from it, placing them carefully on the floor – something she had done hundreds of times before.

He looked at her, expectantly. "And what can I do for you today?"

"I thought we were going to go through the First Rule Day ceremony again, just so I know what to expect."

Realisation dawned on his face. "Oh yes! Of course. I'm so sorry, my dear. This old head of mine..."

He disappeared back into the recesses of dusty tomes and rummaged around for something. She heard more humming as this was going on. After a few seconds, she heard a positive sounding 'Ah!' and Rhowern re-emerged, brandishing an ancient scroll. As old as it was, it was also well looked after and kept in extremely good condition.

"Here we are!" he exclaimed.

With a flourish, and a great deal less care than Evelynn, he swept the books and papers off the other chair and sat down with a thud, as dust motes floated around him like fireflies. Evelynn smiled. He carefully opened the scroll and looked at it.

"Right then," he began. "So, first of all, there will be some speeches by your father. He'll talk a bit about the history of First Rule Day, and when it happened to him and how he felt, blah-de-blah. You know the kind of thing to expect."

She nodded.

"After that," he continued, "the third throne will be brought out. This is all very ceremonious. There'll be some trumpet's blaring and what-not. And then..."

Evelynn sighed. "This is the bit I'm not looking forward too."

Rhowern looked at her with a sympathetic grin. "I know, you're not really one for all the fanfare, but it's an important ceremony and your parents are so proud of you..."

"I know, I know. So, this is where I get put on display."

"That's right. The Royal Announcer will, well, announce you, and you'll rise from where you have been seated in your ceremonial gown, and sit yourself down on the third throne. Then another little speech by the king, and after that he will place upon your head your new crown."

"Is it heavy?" she asked. "I haven't even seen what it looks like."

"Not greatly heavy, no. It's a step up from the tiara you wear as a princess. It's kind of a place-holder crown until the time comes to get the real thing. After that, you will be formally asked if you are prepared to undertake the duties of ruler, should anything happen to your mother and father, and all you have to say is 'I accept'."

"You know, it's weird," she said.

"What is?"

"You'd think I would get asked that BEFORE the crown was put on my head."

Rhowern ruminated on this. "Yes. That does make more sense. Chances are somebody thought of it after the rest had been written down, and they couldn't be bothered to re-do it."

"Even for such an important thing?"

He turned the scroll around so she could see the beautifully detailed intricacies of the writing.

"Are you joking?" he excalaimed. "Look at the penmanship on that! It takes ages!"

4

Flame Peak

If phones had been around on Ethera at the time of this story, chances are that Doran Millar would have used one to call in sick for the day. Or maybe the week.

The little errand on which he had been sent was technically, not dangerous. The dragon, Hargan, hadn't eaten a human (on purpose) for many, many years. And that was in a battle situation. But he was old now. Ancient, in fact, and mistakes can easily be made at that time of life, and Doran didn't fancy being mistaken for a tasty treat. After all, to a dragon as big as Hargan, Doran would be nothing more than a chicken nugget.

Hargan was the last of his kind, and he lived in one of many caves at the top of Flame-Peak, so called because as the sun set every evening, the light made the stone of the mountain shine a vibrant orange. Plus, it was where all the dragons lived, so flames were a daily occurrence. At least, when they were all alive. After the magic had gone, the dragons, which had been in part created by the mystical essence of the universe, had nothing to sustain their life force for longer than maybe a few hundred years. As such, they had slowly, and sadly, started to die off, until only Hargan was left. He had fought on the side of the old king, believing, oddly enough, that humanity should be allowed to flourish and magic to fade. I mean, who would want to live forever? It gets boring after a while. Hargan was bored a lot these days. He only needed to eat once every three days or so, so after devouring a sheep or two, or a horse, or a whale from the oceans, if he was feeling adventurous, the rest of his time was spent doing not much of anything at all.

As he had fought on the side of the old king, Rolannd wanted to invite him as something of a 'guest of honour,' to his daughters First Rule Day. Doran, as one of the kings' guards, had been sent to deliver that message. It was about a day and a half's ride to Flame Peak, and Doran dreaded every moment. The ride made him sore, and the climb at the end of it wasn't going to be much of a picnic.

Then there was the humongous dragon at the end.

Doran could see the peak ahead, coming ever closer. His heart sank.

…

He slowed as he approached the foot of the mountain. Mountain was a bit much, actually. It was more of a very large, rocky hill. He looked up, searching for any sign of his quarry. A large shape peering down at him perhaps, or a flicker of a shadow across the sun. So far, nothing.

Doran slipped his horses reigns over the branch of a spindly tree, then started to make his way up.

Climbing wasn't exactly accurate either. Over the years, rough, stone steps had been hewn into the rock, making the trip a lot less arduous than it could be. Doran still complained though. Inwardly.

He had been told to wear ceremonial armour for the meeting with the dragon *(as if he would care!)* and right now the weight of it was telling on him. Bits of fancy braiding were flapping about his bare knees, and every now and then, on a particularly high step, his metal chest plate would ride up and knock him on the chin. The last two times it happened; Doran ended up biting his tongue. If he didn't get to the top of the steps soon, he feared his tongue would come off altogether.

Finally, the steps opened out onto a much flatter shelf-like area. He could see the entrances to many caves, all once belonging to the dragons of old. All now empty.
Apart from one.

And from that one, a weighty, raspy thrumming emitted.

Hargan's breathing.

He steadied himself and straightened his armour before moving forward toward the dark cave mouth. The nearer he got, the louder it got, so loud, it shook the ground beneath him.

Stopping about twenty feet from the entrance, Doran shouted, in his best regal tones, into the dark abyss, his tongue still swollen by the repeated knocks from his armour.

"Greetingths, oh mighty Hargan. I have come with a methage from King Rolannd of Thayorn to invite you to his daughterths Firtht Rule Day."

Not his best performance, to be sure, but it would do.

As he waited for a reply, he wiped the spit from his chin.

The thrumming was suddenly interrupted by what sounded like a lot of humphs and groans, usually associated with people over fifty waking up in the morning.

The dragons voice when it came, was deep and resonant, and ever so slightly confused.

"WHA…?"

Doran sighed. He cleared his throat and began his speech again.

"Greetingths, oh mighty Hargan! I have come with a methage from…"

"HOLD ON, HOLD ON," came the voice.

Doran heard movement coming from within the cave. It sounded like a rockslide in slow motion.

Gradually, Doran could see, coming out of the darkness of the cave, a gigantic, scaly head, crowned with humongous horns. Teeth protruded from the dragon's mouth, and its body, once a bright, vibrant green, was now dulled with time.

Hargan was impressive alright. But the whole effect was dimmed by the dragon's half-open eyes, still tired from sleep. Or boredom. Before the great beast spoke again, he yawned, revealing a mouth almost the size of another cave in itself, lined with razor sharp teeth – though, Doran noticed, there were just as many gummy gaps as there were teeth.

"NOW THEN," said Hargan. "WHAT'S THIS ABOUT?"

Doran was shaking slightly beneath the gaze of the dragon. Though he was grateful it had recognised him as friend, not foe, so was not going to eat him any time soon. Probably.

Doran repeated his message, but after three times and a still swollen tongue, the regal tone had diminished.

Hargan nodded thoughtfully. "HAPPY TO," he said. "WHEN IS IT?"

"Three days from now," replied Doran.

"I'LL BE THERE" he said.

"Thank you. I thall inform the King immediately."

Doran began to turn away, relieved the meeting was over.

"IF YOU WANT…" began the dragon, "I CAN GIVE YOU A LIFT BACK IF YOU LIKE?"

Doran wasn't sure of the protocol in these matters. He didn't think he should refuse.

But he knew he wasn't going to like it.

Neither was his horse.

5

Nightstone

If the kingdom of Thayorn was a house, then Nighstone castle was a bungalow. Kalem's bungalow, and one he could not wait to move out of.

Nightstone was gifted to Kalem by his father. The castle had earned its name quite simply because the stone from which it was made, was the deepest, darkest black. When, whomever it was, decided to build a castle long centuries ago, they had gone to the nearby mountains to carve the rock and choose suitable stone for its construction, they found, just below the surface, a material of the purest black. As black as night. It was stronger than slate, but duller than obsidian. Being a literal-minded sort, the architect named it nighstone, and gave the name to the castle as well.

Now, all this time later, Kalem called it home. It had an impressive main hall, sweeping corridors, towers, but as impressive as it was, it was also bloody dangerous. When everything is black like that, depth perception goes out the window. Kalem cursed the architect for not including ANY other kind of stone, just for safety purposes. He concluded he must either have been insane or just a sadistic bugger. There had been more than a few accidents when guards or servants had stumbled down the dark steps, totally misjudging the correct place to anchor their feet. And many more of the castle's inhabitants, Kalem included, who had bumped into walls simply because they looked like gloomy entrance ways.

After a while, Kalem had gotten so fed up, he ordered tapestries, pictures and mirrors put up on almost every empty patch of wall, just so people knew exactly where the hell they were going. And most of the stairs got carpeted, too.

...

Kalem could see the castle approaching on the horizon. He was extremely tired, as were his men. The journey out of the Forbidden lands hadn't taken as long, but it was still miserable. The had all managed to find a small lake in which to bathe, trying to get every grain of sand out of every crevice, but there was some still some there.

Lurking.

They could all feel it. The odd unpleasant rub of that gritty, grainy substance scraping against soft, vulnerable skin.

He couldn't wait to have a proper, warm bath. With bubbles.

He was also fed up with the voice coming from the cloth bag tied to his horse, asking what felt like every hour, if they were there yet. He would be glad to answer the question – any minute now – in the affirmative.

...

No sooner had Kalem walked through the doors, his adviser Mylan, swept up to him with a fixed smile and a cheery manner. Most of the time, Kalem found him quite amusing but right now he would happily punch him in the face. He needed those suds.

"Welcome back, my lord! I trust the journey was a productive one."

Mylan was aware of Kalem's objective, but chose, dramatically, to ask the question as if it were a huge secret.

"Yes, it was," he replied.

"Moho his hee?"

Mylan's brow furrowed. He wondered, internally, if Kalem had just practised ventriloquism on him.

"Sire, did you just...?"

"What? Oh, uh, don't worry about that. I'll explain it in a minute. I just need a nice, long bath first. You can tell the servants to get one ready."

"Um, before that, sire..."

Kalem sighed. "What is it?"

"A messenger is here, my lord. From Thayorn. He arrived two days and would not leave here without speaking to you."

"Did he say what the message was about?"

"Not a word. We have had to put him up for two nights."

Kalem sighed again. "Did you tell him where I was?"

"No sire, of course not. We told him you were out hunting."

"Alright then, I'll see him. Here, take this."

He handed the bag containing Rhyfeth's head to Mylan, before grabbing the staff and handing him that, too.

"Take them to my room. And don't open that one. Even if it asks you. And get that bath run!"

Kalem walked toward the main hall, leaving Mylan with his hands full and his face a mask of confusion.

...

The main hall of Nightstone castle was a large black cube, broken up with doorways, tapestries, flaming torches and a roaring fire. The floor had rugs strewn about the place, so that the walker wouldn't second-guess their steps and accidentally fall over.

Kalem had hastily discarded his top layer, flinging it out of sight so that the Royal Messenger would not be able to discern where he might have been. He flung open the main doors and entered like he had just won a hundred battles. His chest was puffed out and his smile was broad.

The messenger was stood by the tapestries, observing the intricate patterns and depictions of what looked like Kalem wrestling with various dangerous animals, like lions and bears, and beating them into submission. Most of them had the Lord of Nightstone standing over the deceased carcasses surrounded by a halo of sunlight, with long flowing hair and a ridiculous macho expression, that looked about as intimidating as a puppy holding a chocolate chip cookie.

The messenger jumped and turned toward the noise. Kalem noticed he was in full ceremonial armour - so it must have been something important.

"G... greetings my lord."

Kalem strolled over to where the messenger was standing. "And what can I do for you?"

"I bring an important message from the King. He asks that I bring back your answer."

"Come on then, let's hear It."

"In two days', time, it is Princess Evelynn's First Rule Day. He has requested your presence for this most important and momentous occasion."

Kalem's brain suddenly exploded. Not literally.

He had already been thinking of some way, some pretext, to go to Thayorn, just so he could somehow get near to the vault, where the orb would no doubt be. And now, thanks to this, he had the perfect reason.

"Tell my brother," He said, pausing dramatically for the revelation to sink in, "I will be there."

The messenger clicked his heels and left.

Kalem remained where he was, ideas bursting like water balloons. *Princess Evelynn, ay?* He hadn't visited his brother and sister-in-law since his little niece was born. *My*, he thought. *How time flies.*

...

After his bath (mmm, bubbles), Kalem wandered freely around his bedroom draped in a loose-fitting robe. He was alone, eyeing the package on his table. He sat, surveying his prize like a child on Christmas morning. He looked at the staff first. The top of it, on closer inspection, looked like the claw of a dangerous bird, opened wide enough to hold a large spherical object. He put it back down on the table and unwrapped the package, revealing the permanently smiling face of Rhyfeth.

"Oh, that's much better," said the skull. "It was stifling in there."

"I didn't think being wrapped in a cloth would bother you, in your current state."

Despite not having a body, the shrug was implied. "I still have feelings."

"Anyway," continued Kalem quickly, "I've just got some news that helps us along no end. It turns out, my niece is having her First Rule Day ceremony in two days' time. I have been invited"

"That's nice."

"Eh? No, you don't understand. Her father, my brother, is king of Thayorn. We are the descendants of Thalra."

"You kept that quiet."

"I didn't want you to think I had any ulterior motive. But you're missing the point." Kalem's voice took on an air of excitement. "The orb will be there! In the vault. All I must do is get into it."

If Rhyfeth could have held his stomach and laughed heartily he would have. Instead, with his skinless head resting on a wooden table, the laugh wheezed out rather pathetically. But it got his point across.

"Excellent," he said. "When the orb and the staff are joined again, I will be able to ta... uh, teach you how to wield it. Then, you will have the power to change the world."

6

The Kingdom of Thayorn

The endeavour to make Doran Miller's life as unbearable as possible continued at an accelerated pace.

And height.

Right now, he was about a mile off the ground, clinging to Hargan's neck for dear life. True, he had lashed himself to the huge beast so as not to fall, but a good grip was just as effective as a piece of knotted rope.

He had his head pressed against the hard scales, tears from the fast moving and chilly air, streaming down his cheeks and drying just as quick as they manifested. Every now and then, he let out a childish whimper, which popped out of his mouth like a train whistle.

Far below, his horse, blindfolded against the terror of its experience, was still neighing uncontrollably. Hargan had a firm hold, keeping the animal secure in his tight, yet yielding grip.

Between Doran and the horse, Hargan was having a good old time. He was giggling, if the word giggling can be attributed to a dragon, at every little noise that Doran and the horse where making. Doran could feel it through the scales – a hefty, broken rumble in the dragon's throat, like a bag of coal rolling down a hill. To Doran, the journey felt like it had taken days, when in fact it was hours.

"THAYORN!" called out Hargan, triumphantly.

Doran's eyes flickered open against the wind, the sight of the magnificent spires and rippling flags blurry through his tears.

"Thank f..." the remainder of the sentiment was lost to the breeze as the dragon picked up speed.

...

In Thayorn, the crowds spotted Hargan approaching. As part of Evelynn's First Rule Day celebrations, and to make Hargan welcome, they had begun working on a landing site for the huge dragon. It was appropriately rocky (dragons preferred a rocky floor to a dirt or grass one, and fancy flags and colourful bunting were being hung all around it.

Unfortunately, as Hargan was so early, the bells and whistles of the site had not yet been finished. Not that anyone had to worry. As long as he had somewhere to rest and a sheep or a cow to munch on, Hargan would be perfectly happy.

...

With an unexpected gentleness Hargan set the horse down first, before landing himself. Immediately some of the stable hands ran forward and led the poor animal away, all of them vowing it would get plenty of sugar lumps and oats for being so brave.

Doran pried his hands off the dragon's neck. He was unsurprised to find his fingers had made dents in the scales. Shakily, he untied the knot that held him to Hargan and slid awkwardly off his perch.
He, too, would probably need some sugar lumps after the ride. And maybe a couple of beers.
Doran looked up at Hargan. He swore the beast was smiling at him.

"Th... thank you," he said, not wanting to seem impolite.

"YOU'RE WELCOME," said Hargan.

The King and Queen, already alert to Hargan's arrival, were approaching in the royal carriage as Doran walked painfully away.

Crowds gathered around, full of excited, but wary adults and children, all of them aware of the existence of dragons, some even having seen them in their time, but never, EVER this close. Hargan was happy enough to be admired.

In a wee corner of the courtyard was a small temple that contained the followers of the main religion of Ailani. Ffhug. The Fhuggees all believed in The Great One and endeavoured to live their lives to the letter of his teachings. They all wore fancy red robes and bright orange hats, which gave them the look of a bunch of candles when they were all stood together. Upon the arrival of the dragon, they got extremely excited and decided to go out and greet him. For Hargan was created by magic, as were all things created by The Great One, and so a creature like Hargan should be worshipped.

However, The Great One also said that magic should be allowed to fade, and humanity should be allowed to rule themselves, so as much as they wanted to worship him, they also had to be 'hands off' and treat him with a kind of mild indifference. All in all, a lot of conflicting and confusing ideas there.

Must be where catholic guilt comes from.

What it resulted in was a line of priests dressed like candles walking hurriedly over to Hargan, smiling, bowing and immediately running back to their temple and crying their eyes out.

...

King Rolannd and Queen Jocelyn also smiled and bowed to the magnificent beast, and Hargan bowed his head in acknowledgement.

"We are so glad you accepted our invitation, mighty Hargan," began Rolannd. "Though we didn't expect you so early. I hope you are happy with your, uh, area."

"ITS PERFECTLY FINE, THANK YOU. I THOUGHT I WOULD MAKE AN EARLY START OF IT. THERE'S ONLY SO MUCH TO LOOK AT INSIDE A CAVE, YOU KNOW. AND I WANTED TO MEET THE PRINCESS."

"I'll send for her immediately," said Jocelyn.

But there was no need. Evelynn was well aware of the excitement and came running through the crowd to see the dragon she had heard so much about. She had never seen a dragon before, at all. Only pictures, so her face was a mask of wonder.

"W... wow. You're amazing," she said.

The pale green scales on Hargan's face seemed to flush and go a little red.

"THANK YOU," he replied. "YOU'RE NOT SO BAD YOURSELF."

7

The Edge of the Darkwood

Kalem had dressed in his finest for the journey to Thayorn. He had two men with him, Pax and Beck, both his personal guard. All three wore armour that had been polished to a high shine. Like everything connected with Nightstone, their outfits were predominantly black, though Kalem had them edged with silver.

Befitting his hero status (even though he had conferred it to himself), Kalem wore a lot of leather, which, as he rode along on his saddle, made a sound like two balloons rubbing together.

In order to get to Thayorn from Nightstone, the three had to journey a considerable way around the Darkwood. That forest was to be avoided at all costs, even though it would have stripped almost a day off their journey time.

The Darkwood was home to a lot of rather nasty, vindictive creatures. Scummy, vile monsters that liked nothing better than to cause harm. Tax Collectors would probably like it there.

Lots of trolls lived in the Darkwood. There are all kinds of trolls. Some are made of stone and can only move about at night. Some are big, bear-like creatures, all hair and drool, who enjoy living under bridges.

The trolls in the Darkwood were all about five feet high, with sharp clawlike fingers and pointy ears. Their faces had a monkey-like appearance, but with more angular features. Their lower teeth jutted far out past their flat snouts, and the hair that covered their bodies was always matted and greasy.

Oh, and they liked eating flesh. Any flesh, but human was their favourite. Given that most (smart) humans avoided the forest like the plague, the trolls hardly ever got to eat human flesh. But on occasion, maybe a travelling merchant from across the sea, or some idiot drunkard with no sense of direction, would stumble into the Darkwood. And never stumble out again. The trolls lived in the trees and attacked from above. They enjoyed shade and shadow, and hated the sun, so would never venture out beyond the tree line.

Kalem, Pax and Beck eyed the trees as they passed them – at a very safe distance. Even know, black crows circled and wheeled overhead, cawing mercilessly. Kalem couldn't help but shiver. Perched on his saddle was the skull of Rhyfeth. Kalem had tied it on securely, facing him, so they could talk on their way to Thayorn. Kalem had… introduced the semi-dead wizard to the people of Nightstone to get them used to him. Apart from one or two fainting servants and some funny looks, it all seemed to go well. Kalem turned away from the Darkwood and carried on his conversation.

"As I was saying," he continued, "I know where the vault is, but I don't have the key. I may have to threaten someone for it. Unless you can get us in?"

Kalem looked hopefully down at the empty skull in front of him.

"Until I am face to face with the orb, I can do nothing. When that happens, I can get us out of there quick enough. Like lightning. But as for getting in – that's your headache."

Kalem sighed. *Why does everything have to be so difficult?* he thought.

"We'll manage it," he said aloud.

"And when you get the orb, remember what I said we have to do." said Rhyfeth.

"You want me to say a spell."

"No, *we* must say the spell. Together, as one. When we do that, I will be able to pass control of the magic directly to you."

Kalem smiled at that part. "So, I alone will have control of all the magic on Ethera."

"That's exactly right," said Rhyfeth. "Exactly right indeed."

Had the skull possessed an actual face, Kalem may have noticed subtle hints and clues that Rhyfeth was not to be totally trusted. Like a creepy smile, or a widening of the eyes. As it was, the lord of Nightstone thought only of his own future glory, not realising for a moment that the wizard was thinking of exactly the same thing.

8

The Kingdom of Thayorn

Night was drawing in, and Princess Evelynn sat next to her window, looking out at the stars. If this was from Disney, now would be the time for a song.

Her First Rule Day was the day after tomorrow. She was nervous, excited, anxious, all the biggies, but more than anything, she just didn't want to mess up.

Her parents had been so good to her and had allowed her to grow up into the person she wanted to be. They hadn't closeted her, hadn't hid her away. When she wanted to go out and greet the people, she was allowed to. Anything she wanted to try, as long as it wasn't bungee jumping into an active volcano, was fine by them. But ruling a kingdom was a big deal. And the First Rule celebrations told her that, in big gold letters and on fluttering banners. Would she be a good ruler? She'd like to think so.

She wanted to make her parents proud - and she wanted to make herself proud too.

...

The first rays of the sun are often accompanied by the crow of a rooster. But as the day dawned in Thayorn, it was accompanied by the roar of a dragon, yawning, and the scrabble of all sorts of farm animals, roosters included, running for cover.

It was the kings turn to ponder next to a window today and ponder he did. He was wondering if Kalem was actually going to show up. His messenger had reported that he was, but with Kalem, you never knew. He had to come today to be ready for the celebration tomorrow, but then again, knowing his brother, he could deliberately arrive in the middle of it all, just to draw all the attention onto him and away from Evelynn.

The king sighed. It had been so long since they had spoken. Kalem had only seen Evelynn once, as a baby, and had never bothered to drop in since to see how she was doing.

Rolannd was well aware how strained his relationship with Kalem was. Kalem wanted to be king. Felt he deserved it. Felt he could have done a better job. Rolannd shook his head, sadly. He couldn't help being first born. That's just the way it was. Rolannd would even have been happy to let Kalem sit on the Royal Council, but for two things. One, Kalem thought it wasn't enough. And two, he was an idiot. Well, not the 'oh dear I've put my trousers on back-to-front' kind of idiot, but he had no mind for being a great ruler. Or a sensible one.

He wanted it *his* way. Thought all the attention should be on *him*. And that's not what being a king is all about. Rolannd was so glad Evelynn wasn't like her uncle. She was so much more grounded. And real. And sensible.

He sighed again.

It was that kind of day.

...

About two miles away from the kingdom, Kalem, Pax and Beck approached on their horses. They had woken early, breakfasted, and started on their merry way. Kalem could see the huge spires in the distance. He felt his lip curling into a sneer.

"You alright?" Asked Rhyfeth. "You look like you stepped in something."

"Just getting nearer that's all. Nearer to him. Oh, I could just slap him in the face."

"Now just settle down," said Rhyfeth. "If you go in there with an attitude like that, we won't get anywhere near the vault. He'll just tell you to naff off and never comes back."

"I know, I know," conceded Kalem.

"I am not saying you have to be all sweetness and light. Given what you've told me, that would just make him suspicious. But you must be careful. Cool, calm and collected."

Kalem had to agree. He had been planning for so long how to become ruler of Thayorn, he couldn't let the best chance he had slip through his fingers now, when he was so close.

"Alright," he said, finally. "Come on then. Let's get this over with. I'll have to put you away."

Rhyfeth also had to concede the unpleasant truth that for the next few hours at least, he would have to go back in the bag.

...

There was very little fanfare for Kalem's arrival.

Given as no one knew exactly when he was coming, that wasn't surprising, but still, he wouldn't have minded a bit of acknowledgement from the people as he rode through them toward the castle. A couple of Royal guards spotted Kalem, or more specifically, the fancy armour, and decided to rush off to the castle to pass on the news.

By the time Kalem and his men got there, Rolannd and Jocelyn were waiting. A long, scarlet-red carpet had been unrolled like a tongue out of the main entrance. Despite his thinking, the carpet had not been unrolled especially for him, rather it was there ready for the First Rule Day celebrations. But Kalem smiled at the thought anyway.

Jocelyn kept a neutral and indifferent look on her face, but Rolannd couldn't help but get a little excited. Despite everything, he was happy to see his brother, and hoped Kalem would feel the same way.

"Kalem! Brother! I'm so glad you accepted my... uh, our invitation."

Jocelyn's nose twitched.

Kalem dismounted, while Pax and Beck remained on their horses, watching. He walked slowly over to Rolannd, who sped toward his brother, his arms outstretched.

"I'm so glad to see you. It's been so long."

"It has indeed. Brother."

Kalem allowed Rolannd to wrap his arms around him. Reluctantly, he raised his own arms and returned the embrace. Catching Jocelyn's eye, he made sure to smile, though it looked more like a grimace.

After what felt like an eternity, Rolannd let go. He placed his hands on Kalem's shoulders and looked into his brother's eyes. "We should not have let it go on so long. You should have come to visit sooner."

"Or you could have come to visit me, right?"

There was a hint of acid in Kalem's words that the king, reluctantly, had to agree with.

"You are right. But ruling a kingdom, raising a daughter, it... it takes up a lot of time."

Kalem let a pair of stony eyes rest on his brother's face.

Rolannd nodded. "But you are right. I should have come. I could have. But come now, can we not start anew?"

Kalem's eyes softened. "Yes. Let us... start anew."

Rolannd smiled widely. "Good. Good!"

Jocelynn smiled at them both, though it lacked conviction. Rolannd guided Kalem into the castle. Before he walked through the door, he turned back to Beck and Pax, giving a slight nod. That was the queue to take their horses to the stables and find rooms.

The vast interior of the castle was like a wide-open sky compared to Nightstone's cramped little cube. Long, flowing flags hung between wide stone pillars, long, thin stain-glass windows let in colour-streaked light. Jealousy filled Kalem's throat and threatened to pour out of his mouth, but he kept it down.

"We shall have to introduce you to Evelynn," said Jocelyn, trying to be civil. "She's all grown up now."

"So, I gather. When the messenger told me it was her First Rule Day, I was fairly shocked."

"As were we," said Jocelyn. "Time flies, it seems."

"It does," replied Kalem, out loud. *Unless you are waiting for something, then it is a slow, painful crawl.*

...

Evelynn was curious about her uncle. She had heard of him, of course. And she had heard the way her mother had spoken about him. When she finally came face to face with him, she was civil and polite. Kalem was polite in return. It seemed to Evelynn that Kalem was constantly looking for somewhere to lean. And every now and then he would shake his head to display his black locks like a peacock would display its feathers.

His arrival had made her father happy, so she was happy. Her mother looked like she was just about tolerating the whole thing. Evelynn just hoped that her First Rule Day would pass without a hitch, and that Kalem would go on his way again afterward.

9

That night, Rolannd invited Kalem to dinner.

The king and queen sat at the head of the table, with Evelynn on her father's right, and Kalem on the queen's left. Another place was set, but as yet, no one occupied it.

As the food was brought in, Rolannd tried to make small talk with his brother. However, much like visiting relatives in hospital, it dried up within about half a minute. When the king asked him "what have you been up to for the last decade or so," Kalem simply answered, "not much."

Evelynn tried to save the day by asking about Kalem's home.

"I've heard so much about Nightstone," she said.

"Really? What kind of things have you heard?"

"That the stone is of the purest, deepest black on earth."

Kalem nodded. "True enough."

"It must be fascinating to live in a place made entirely out of such stone."

"Only if you like concussion."

It was then they heard some melodious humming coming from the hallway outside, and then Rhowern entered.

"Evening all," he said cheerfully. "Sorry I'm late."

Rhowern plonked himself onto his seat and Rolannd gave a subtle nod to the servants that the meal could now be served. As plates and cutlery clanked and clanged, Kalem eyed the old man with malice.

"Are you still alive? I thought you'd be dead by now. If not from age, then from a heart attack."

Rhowern did not bat an eye at the insult, instead, he took it all in good cheer. "No lad. Still plodding on."

"And are you still peddling all that nonsense you did with me and him? Whatsisname?"

"Education."

"Yeah, that."

"I am indeed. And clearly you didn't keep up with yours."

Stifling a laugh, Evelynn quickly interjected.

"Rhowern is teaching me. I find it all really interesting."

"Yeah, well," began Kalem, "you have to say that. The old fart is sitting right there."

"No, I do!" I love learning all about maths and history. It's fascinating."

As the food was laid out, Kalem shook his head sadly. *The youth of today*, he thought.

...

The rest of the meal played out in strained silence and broken pieces of awkward conversation. When it was over, they wished each other a clipped goodnight and went their separate ways.

Evelynn found herself walking behind Rhowern, who, instead of his usual cheery humming, was murmuring quietly.

"Are you alright?" she asked.

He turned. "Oh, princess! I didn't see you there. Yes… I'm fine. Just, thinking."

"Can you tell me why things between my father and uncle are so… strained?"

Rhowern stopped walking and they both regarded each-other. He sighed.

"Jealousy, my dear. It's nothing more than that. Kalem was always jealous of your father. Jealous that he was to become king, which I suppose is fair enough. But he would always accuse your father of cheating at games, or getting a bigger slice of cake, of being taller, even."

"But surely, they love each other though, right?" she asked. "They are brothers after all."

Rhowern sighed again. "The problem, my dear, is that jealousy can be just as strong as love in the minds of some. And like love, it can make us say and do some pretty stupid things. I remember I knew this woman named Buxom Bertha and…"

Rhowern suddenly remembered who he was talking to. "Never mind. Look don't let things bother you. You have a big day tomorrow."

She nodded.

"Now, goodnight my dear. And sleep tight."

"Goodnight, Rhowern."

...

Kalem went back to his room, where Beck and Pax were waiting. Pax held a familiar cloth bag, which was currently mumbling to itself.

"Is hne mack net?"

"What was that?" asked Kalem.

Pax let the cloth fall away from the grinning skull. "I said, is he back yet. And here you are. So, let's get on with it."

"Let's wait an hour. Let everyone get settled in their own rooms. Then we'll go to the vault."

"What do we do if we come across any guards?" asked Beck.

"I remember this place pretty well. There are some nooks and crannies we can hide in. But if we have to hurt them... then so be it."

"When you say hurt, do you mean...?" Beck slid his finger across his throat in the universal sign of 'make dead.' He did it with a leery smile.

Kalem considered this for a moment, then nodded in the affirmative. "If we have to, then yes."

...

While Rolannd and Jocelyn settled into their bed, Rolannd telling himself that the meeting with his brother had gone 'swimmingly', Evelynn lay restless, her silken sheets knotted and twisted around her. It was a big day tomorrow. The First Rule Day ceremony. Despite lots of positive encouragement from Rhowern and her parents, she was still dreading it. All the pomp and faffing about. It wasn't her style. She let it play over and over in her head, hoping – and praying to the Great One – that she wouldn't mess it up. After about half an hour of this, she got fed up and decided to go for a walk.

...

The hour was up, and Kalem, Pax and Beck crept as stealthily as they could out of the room. Rhyfeth was with them, carried in his cloth hammock, swaying back and forth like a bag of marbles. With (a quite unnecessary) finger to his lips to indicate silence, Kalem led them towards the stairs that would lead them up to the next floor – to the vault.

Evelynn was just turning a corner when she saw the three men tiptoeing ridiculously away from her.

Intrigued, she followed.

10

The door that led to the stairs was, thankfully, unguarded. As Beck kept a look out for any unwanted spectators, Kalem opened the door. It swung on its hinges with a quiet squeak, which was only slightly louder than a mouses fart. Peering in, he saw the steps leading upward, the way lit by a flaming torch. Beckoning to his men, they started on their way, Beck closing the door behind them. Evelynn saw them go. She stepped out of her shadowy hiding place and walked up to the door, pressing her ear against it. She couldn't hear anything. No footsteps. Nothing. She let a minute pass, more than enough time for the three men to make it to the next floor. As stealthily as possible, Evelynn opened the door as little as possible, and squeezed her wiry frame though the gap. The torch lit an empty stairway.

She walked up, closing the door behind her.

...

Behind Evelynn, another figure watched. One who also couldn't sleep. It wasn't to do with the ceremony. It was to do with a feeling. An unpleasant feeling, that Kalem was up to no good. As quietly as he could, Rhowern waddled up to the door, full of concern now, not only because he was worried about what Kalem was doing, but about Evelynn, and what may happen should she be caught. He thought about his options and decided on a course of action.

...

The vault was the vault because it had a big, round metal door. It didn't have a combination to get into it, but it did have two locks, either side of a metal wheel that had to be turned in order for the door to open. The keys for the locks were held by the two guards who stood outside it. Both keys were necessary.

Kalem peered around the corner and spied the two guards. They both looked like they had had a long day. One of them yawned. Kalem could see the keys dangling from chains around their necks. There were two flaming torches either side of the vault door, making the shadows dance all around them. Kalem emerged from behind the corner and walked up to the guards. They immediately became alert.

"Who goes there?" Asked one.

"Don't you recognise the king's brother when you see him?" Said Kalem. "I have every right to be here and... uh... ah, forget it."

As quick as a flash, Kalem drew his sword and buried the blade into one of the guard's stomachs. As the other guard unsheathed his own sword, Pax rushed to Kalem's side and thrust his own weapon into the man's chest. Pax looked to his lord, questioningly.

"I thought we weren't going to hurt anybody if we didn't have to."

Kalem shrugged. "I just couldn't be bothered waiting anymore."

"Fair enough."

"Get his key."

Pax bent down and grabbed the key that was hanging around the guard's neck, while Kalem grabbed the other one.

"Where is Beck?"

Before anyone could answer, Beck emerged from the shadows, his right arm clasped tightly around Evelynn's body, his other hand covering her mouth.

"Look what I found." he said.

...

The moment Kalem was stabbing a guard in the stomach, Evelynn had climbed the stairs and pushed her body against the wall. She was completely in the darkness, out of the range of the torch light. Beck was slightly ahead of her, his body tense and waiting to pounce. An involuntary yelp escaped her lips when she saw the blood pour from beneath the guard's armour. The moment Pax stabbed the other guard, she was turning away to run back down the stairs.

That was when Beck turned and grabbed her out of the shadows.

...

"Well, well. Look who we have here," said Kalem, in a mocking tone. "A pretty little hostage." He looked at Beck. "Keep hold of her."

After about three minutes of working out the turning the keys/turning the wheel first combo, the vault door swung open. The metal hinges squealed from lack of use. Kalem and Pax walked into the large, round room. It was circular in shape, with no windows at all. Pax grabbed a torch off the wall outside and stood next to his master. The flickering flame highlighted piles of gold and jewels- the kingdoms wealth.

Kalem wasn't interested in any of that, though Pax nabbed a swift handful and put it in his pocket. As the gold glittered and shone, Kalem took hold of Rhyfeth's skull, using him like a laser pointer.

"Is it here? Can you sense it?"

"It's here, alright. I can feel it." Even Rhyfeth couldn't hide his excitement. "There! Straight ahead!"

Kalem beckoned to Pax and they both moved forward. One of them knocked a pile of coins and heard them tinkle and fall. As the torch lit their way, they finally came upon a large wooden chest, almost hidden by a mound of gold coins.

"It's in there."

Kalem brushed the coins away and looked down at the box.

The chest did not have a lock on it. Kalem reached out and lifted the lid. It fell back with a clatter, and for a moment, both men gritted their teeth at the loud noise. Inside was a large round football sized orb. Glistening like glass, with a silver, pearl-like sheen. It reflected in Kalem's eyes like a full moon in the night sky.

"It's beautiful," said Kalem, awestruck by the sight.

Even now, just lying there in a wooden box, the orb seemed to vibrate with energy. They could all feel it.

Especially Rhyfeth.

The hollow eye sockets in his head glowed with white light. "At last."

Suddenly, there was a shout from outside the vault, and Beck rushed in, still holding the struggling Evelynn in his vice-like grip.

"What is it?" shouted Kalem.

Before he had a chance to answer, the vault was filled with the light of more torches, as Rolannd, Rhowern, Captain Greeve and two other guards flooded in. Rolannd saw his daughter, panic-stricken and struggling in Beck's arms.

"What is the meaning of this?" he hissed at his brother. "Let my daughter go at once."

Kalem smiled. "Or what?"

He held up a still bloody blade to Evelynn's throat.

"Or what? *Brother*?" He spat the word.

"Is it money you want?" pleaded Rolannd, his tone softer now, unsure of what Kalem was planning to do. "Take it. Take it all! Just let her go."

"No, I don't think I will. She may come in handy."

"So, what is it then? What do you want?"

Kalem picked up the orb and held it up.

It took a moment for Rolannd to recognise what it was, the orb having been locked up for years and years. Even before he was born. Rhowern, however, student of history that he was, knew immediately.

His eyes widened. "Oh, no!"

"What do I want, dear brother?" said Kalem, his eyes narrowing to vicious slits. "Everything."

Beside them, placed on a mound of gold coins, Rhyfeth uttered a single word. "Clundoor..." and in a flash of light, Kalem, Beck, Pax, Evelynn, Rhyfeth and the orb, all disappeared.

Rolannd watched, dumbfounded, unsure of what had happened or what to say.

Rhowern was more pragmatic.

"We're in pretty deep shit," he said.

PART TWO

11

Nightstone

Kalem paced back and forth excitedly. He had the orb, he had the staff, and as a deterrent against his brother trying some all-out attack, he had Evelynn, locked in a cell down below. If he had been any more excited, there was a very real risk he would have wet himself.

At this moment, the staff and the orb, not yet reunited, were sitting on the table in Kalem's room. Every now and then, Kalem would cease his pacing and look down lovingly at the magical object, shiny and glistening, like a huge pearl.

"Did you see their faces!" he exclaimed. "When we just disappeared. Oh, it was glorious. If only there was a way to capture that look forever. I would frame it and place it on my wall."

He was, of course, talking to Rhyfeth, who was also on the table. He had been listening to Kalem's self-congratulatory proclamations for what seemed like an age. Now, he just wanted to get on with it.

"So, are you ready?" he asked finally.

Kalem stepped up to the table and looked down into Rhyfeth's hollow eyes. "Yes. Yes, I'm ready."

"Good."

"Only..."

Rhyfeth sighed. His patience was running short. "Only what?"

"This spell thing. What if I mess it up?" Kalem's face screwed up into a look of petulance that his parents had no doubt seen every day of his youth.

"You can't mess it up," said Rhyfeth. "You've been practising it haven't you?"

"Yeah..."

"Exactly as I taught you?"

"Uh-huh."

"Then you'll be fine."

"But what if I say a word wrong? It won't destroy the world or anything, will it?"

Rhyfeth sighed inwardly. "You won't destroy the world. You just have to say the words exactly the same time as I say them. Rydyn nin dawr yn rhun. Repeat that."

Kalem's brow furrowed with the effort. "Rydyn nin dawr rhun."

"Good. Now, first things first. Take hold of the staff and place the orb upon it."

Kalem did as he was told. He picked up the staff and held it tightly. Then he picked up the orb with his other hand. Looking into its depths, it was as if all of time was happening at once. It showed everything, yet it showed nothing. Brief flashes of light and energy, then pure white clouds of nothing at all. As he drew the objects together, they both hummed with a relentless energy. A build-up of power, like water behind a weakening dam.

When the orb was placed at the top of the staff, they seemed drawn together like a magnet, and the glass object hit the claw-like shape with a ting sound that reverberated around the entire room. An invisible wind began to blow, swirling all around Kalem's body. He laughed nervously, his heart pounding like a hammer striking an anvil.

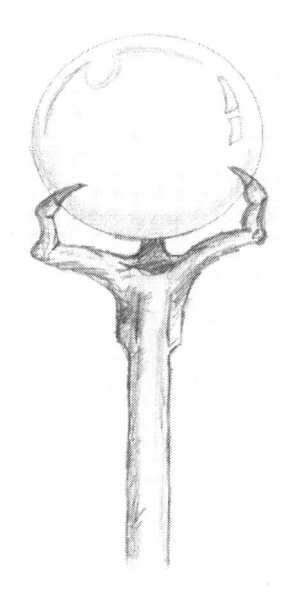

Rhyfeth spoke, but his voice had changed. It seemed deeper, and more defined.

"Now, are you ready?" he asked.

"Re... ready!"

"Remember, we say the spell at the same time!"

"I know, I know."

"After three. One... two..."

"Give me a second."

"What's the hold up."

"I just needed a second, that's all."

"So, are you ready now?"

"Ready."

"Okay. One... two...three..."

Kalem took a breath and started.

"Rydyn nin da... do... oh bugger."

"Rydyn nin dawr...oh, come on!"

"Sorry. I just got a bit flustered. Let's do it again. After three. One, two three... Rydyn nin..."

"Hold on, I wasn't ready that time."

"Shit."

"Let me count down."

"Why can't I count down?"

"It's better if I do it."

"I don't see why."

"It just is."

"Fine."

"AND GET IT RIGHT!"

"Right."

"One... two... three..."

"Rydyn nin dawr yn rhun."

"Rydyn nin dawr yn rhun."

"Haha!" shouted Kalem, triumphantly. "I got it right."

"Yes," said Rhyfeth, the sinister smile implied. **"You did."**

A bright, blinding flash shone out from the orb, and Kalem's body stiffened, as if frozen. In a split second, the light faded, and the wind stopped. Rhyfeth's skull was now... just a skull. His soul was no longer tethered to it. Now, he had tethered himself to something a lot more malleable. And moveable.

Kalem's eyes were tight shut. His last act as his own man. When they opened, it was Rhyfeth who looked out. The spell he had cunningly taught to Kalem was a soul spell. In other words, it gave the soul the power to enter and control another's body. But the other had to agree to it, hence, saying the spell in tandem. Kalem's soul was still in there. Somewhere. But now it occupied a lesser space. Like a butt-cheek or maybe a big toe.

When he spoke, it was still in Kalem's voice, but the tone had changed. It was stricter. Stronger. A bit more no-nonsense than before. Rhyfeth danced – *actually danced* around the room, upon legs that he had missed for centuries, smiling and laughing at his cleverness. When he stopped, he looked upon the staff, the orb set firmly on top of it.

"And now, at last, magic will return to the world and be used in the only way it should be. My way."

...

Down in the dungeon, Evelynn sat on a pile of damp straw and contemplated her situation. For one, she couldn't believe her uncle – *her own uncle* – had kidnapped her and stuck her in this damp and dusty cell.

Second, the magic. Magic had transported them from the vault all the way back to Nightstone in the blink of an eye. It had been quite a thrill. To be enveloped in light, and then suddenly feel like your entire body had no substance at all, just for a split second, and then *whoomp!* Back to normal. Magic had been unheard of in the world for years and years, and now, suddenly, it was back. And the very key to it, it seemed, was in the vault all along.

She started to think about how to get out of her current predicament. No easy task, given the heavy metal bars set into the doorway, and the rather large guard outside. Maybe she could appeal to his sensitive side.

"Excuse me," she said, softly. "Could I have some water please?"

"Shut up, maggot."

Or maybe not.

12

The Kingdom of Thayorn

Rolannd walked around and around the council chamber until the men seated at the table were almost dizzy. Captain Greeve and Rhowern stayed silent as their king ranted and exclaimed, giving him the chance to get the irrationalities out of the way before starting the real planning.

Jocelyn was in her bed chamber, inconsolable and angry, wanting immediate action. When Rolannd told her she had to be patient and allow them to plan, a rather dangerous glint appeared in her eye, one which told him that retreat was the best option. The second best was to leave her alone and not go back to see her until a plan had been formed.

"How could he have done this?" said Rolannd, for what was maybe the tenth time. "I'm his brother. His own brother. Kidnapping my daughter. His own flesh and blood. Of all the low down, underhanded... and how do we get her back? I'll tell you how. We'll march the whole bloody army to that traitor's castle and take it down a piece at a time until we get her back, that's what..."

It was wise for Greeve and Rhowern to keep their more sensible opinions and questions to themselves at this moment, so they just eyed each-other, helplessly.

Finally, Rolannd stopped walking and turned to them both. "Well, come on! Have either of you got anything to say?"

He walked over to his seat at the head of the table and sat angrily in it (if that is even possible).

Greeve cleared his throat. "While I agree that we must get the princess back as quickly and safely as possible, my lord, we must also remember that Kalem has the orb. He has the most concentrated source of magic anywhere in the world."

"And sire," interrupted Rhowern, "if you were to march on him in force, it's quite probable that he would harm Evelynn in some way."

"I would like to think that he would not go so far," said Rolannd, sadly. "But you are probably right. And all that magic in his hands. But can he even use it?"

It should be said that none of them noticed the skull of Rhyfeth in the vault.

"It seems to me," said Greeve, "that your brother has been planning this for some time. Maybe he has learned."

The words hung in the air.

"So how do I get my daughter back?"

More silence.

"What if..." began Rhowern, "we do nothing."

"Groundbreaking stuff."

"No, no. We only look like we are doing nothing. Kalem will probably expect an army to march to Nightstone, so if no army appears, he'll be wondering what on Ailani we are doing."

Captain Greeve looked at the plump old man. "And what are we doing?"

"Well, a full army on the march would take a few days to get there, right?"

"Right."

"And if Kalem is looking for that, he won't be expecting the much smaller force to come at him from the rear. As it were."

"And that would be…"

"We send a small team through the Darkwood."

Rolannd jumped up. "The Darkwood? But it's dangerous in there! They might be killed."

"Exactly! No one would be expecting them to come from that direction. And if they set off soon, they'll get there in no time at all."

Rolannd looked at Greeve. "What do you think?"

Greeve sighed. "Well, it will be exceptionally dangerous. I'd have to send my best men, fully armed. It could only be a small group, mind. The smaller, the quicker. With the element of surprise, they could make it into Nightstone unseen."

"Ah," interjected Rhowern, "I can help even further with that. Upstairs, I have the architect plans for Nightstone. Including sewer systems."

Greeve smiled. "That sounds good. If we can get in that way, it shouldn't be much of a problem getting the princess out the same way. I think we can do it."

"Alright then. My wife will be relieved to know we have a plan. So, tell me, Captain, who do you have in mind?"

13

82

The whole kingdom was now aware of Evelynn's kidnapping. Rumour and speculation were rampant. Who did it? Why? Plenty enough thought it was Kalem. Like all good subjects, they were completely immersed in gossip, and knew that the king and his brother were not on the best of terms. And no one had seen 'the brother' since. Then of course, was the other rumour. The one about magic. There had been whispers of sorcery being used to magic the princess away.

Would it be war?

Ransom?

In Thayorn, there was no better place for speculation than a little pub, nestled snuggly into a quiet corner.

Known as The Wizard's Tipple, the sign – an upside-down wizard's hat filled with booze – was always bright and gleaming. Mostly because the landlord needed to repaint it on a weekly basis, as some of the cheekier youngsters in the kingdom liked to replace the 't' in tipple with an 'n.'
It was evening now, and several royal guards sat in the corner of the pub, drinking ale, and mumbling about the possibilities of war, or perhaps some other notion of getting the princess back.

They liked the princess. She was always kind and funny and amazingly easy to relate to. They wanted to get her back, too. They just wondered how it could be done. Maybe they would try a rescue? No doubt they would find out soon enough.

Doran Millar contemplated with the rest of them. He sat on a seat of his own, a soft cushion beneath him. The aches and pains from riding Hargan were starting to subside, so he wouldn't need the cushion much longer. Though he had grown used to it. Doran had a mix of emotions. He, too, liked the princess a great deal. And he wanted her back, safe and sound. But he also thought *'hey, I've travelled all the way to Flame Peak, I returned on the back of a dragon. I've DONE my bit.'*

Unfortunately for Doran, those fantastic feats just made him sound to the higher-ups, to be the *perfect* man for the job.

All around the inn, the hustle and bustle of murmured conversation and clattering tankards, spilt drinks, and bursts of high (inebriated) emotion were going on as usual.

When suddenly, they stopped. Stopped dead, like a closed door in someone's face. Heads were turning toward the door. Doran and the other guards all turned too.

In the doorway stood Captain Greeve, in full armour, looking *very* serious. He was scanning the room, his eyes moving slowly. He knew EXACTLY who he was looking for.

So did Doran. Deep down. He knew where those eyes would stop. Inside, his heart sunk to somewhere around his ankles.

He locked eyes with the captain.

Greeve smiled and walked over to where Doran and the guards were sitting. They all stood to attention at Greeve's approach. He gave them all an official nod then focussed on Doran.

"Evening, Millar," said Greeve.

"Sir."

"I have a job for you."

...

Religion is a confusing thing at the best of times, and recently in Thayorn, for the Ffhugees, it had become most confusing indeed. Promoting the words of The Great One meant believing completely that magic was not the way to go. It was out of the picture. Gone. Snuffed, supposedly, out of all existence. And that's the way it should be. That's what it said in the Great Book, and that's the way it was.

The problem is words on a page can be misinterpreted. Twisted. Altered. And so it was, now that magic was back in the picture, many Ffhugees started to think perhaps that The Great One was merely testing humanity. Just to see how well they could cope without magic, and then suddenly bring it back. Dangle it like a carrot. Does humanity need magic? Does it deserve it? Has it been brought back just because that's the way it should be and that's how The Great One wants it?

As with all this religion stuff, there were no concrete answers, just faith. But anyone who has every waited for a bus in bad weather knows, faith is not always enough.

They had started to argue amongst themselves, though for the Ffhugees, the arguments weren't particularly aggressive. They were a peaceful religious organisation (weren't they all?) and didn't believe in violence. As such, most of the arguments descended rather quickly into childish name-calling and storming off. To be honest, though, some of the arguments had resulted in brief outbursts of aggression. Though a bit of limp-wristed arm-flailing could hardly be perceived as violence. One of the priests slapped himself in the eye and another got a splinter when he swung his arm too wide and hit a wooden pillar.
Eventually, it led to more tears and apologies, though some of the apologies were not as genuine as they needed to be, leading to a bit of resentment and unspoken thoughts of vengeance, which entailed catching a frog to put in their enemy's bed.

The High Priest of the Ffhugees, also known as Kevin, preached peace and togetherness, and offered a general piece of advice to all the members of the church, which amounted to 'grow up you bunch of dingbats.'

After such a harsh admonishment, (which even Kevin couldn't believe he had delivered, needing a stiff cranberry juice afterward to settle his nerves) the Ffhugees decided to put aside their differences and meditate on The Great One's great purpose.

Even though it was confusing as hell.

Not having a solid answer or direction was confusing and unsatisfying, and each of them hoped that Kevi... uh, the High Priest, would not ask them directly for their honest opinion, which could lead to them spontaneously combusting on the spot. In the end, they went to their beds unhappy and unfulfilled, which ended, as with most things lately, in more tears.

14

Nightstone

Rhyfeth had done a pretty good job of convincing everyone in the castle that he was Kalem. In all honesty, they didn't take much convincing. Kalem used to spend his time wandering the halls and chatting up the servant girls. Now he had magic, his followers supposed, Kalem's focus had now changed. He was busy making plans. He seemed so much more mature, even a little dangerous. But they remained satisfied that this was their master.

Everyone except Mylan.

He had been closer to Kalem than anyone. He had had to stay up until all hours listening to his masters relentless plotting to overthrow his brother, how his parents never thought he would amount to much, how much nicer Thayorn was to Nightstone, how he was going to go to the Forbidden Lands and find a thingy... he had heard it all. So, this sudden change didn't sit well with Mylan.

Not one bit.

...

It was dinner time, and Kalem was in the main hall tucking into a rather large roast chicken. That was another thing, Kalem had lost his appetite and found an elephant's, attacking each of his meals with vigour.

Mylan crept around the hallways toward his master's room. It felt odd, creeping around like this, when usually he would be walking these halls with open pride. He reached Kalem's bedroom door and reached out toward the handle.

Suddenly, there was a burst of laughter from down below. That was yet *another* thing. Kalem had found a brand-new sense of humour. Before, the laughter from his men would be forced and unnatural – more of the 'if you don't laugh at my puerile humour, I'll rip your nuts off' kind of thing. Now, the laughter from below was a genuine, hearty guffaw. It wasn't right.

It wasn't right at *all*.

Mylan turned the handle to the bedroom door and slipped quietly in.

The room looked like a hurricane had hit it. Maps, clothes, bedsheets, all strewn about the place with no rhyme or reason. Mylan closed the door behind him and stepped fully into the room, looking about the place for something, anything, that would explain what was going on.

And then he found it.

Rhyfeth's skull.

It was placed on the table, as it had always been. Even though it was a skull, it always seemed to have a sense of life about it. That genuine, human thoughts were going on within those hollow sockets.

Now, there seemed to be... nothing.

Mylan walked right up to the desk and looked down at it.

"Uh... um... hello?"

Nothing happened.

He poked the skull, ever so quickly. He didn't want it to bite him. Perhaps it was just asleep.

Nothing.

He poked it again.

Nothing.

Mylan was smarter than his master. That wasn't him being big-headed, it was just fact, so putting two plus two together didn't take a whole lot of time. He knew what had happened. He didn't know *how*, but he knew *what*.

And that's when the bedroom door opened.

Mylan jumped and turned at the same time, like some kind of toy spring. He saw Kalem standing there, a wicked smile on his face. In his right hand he held the magical staff. He was never without it now. Ever.

"You... you're not Kalem," blurted Mylan.

"And what makes you say that?" said Kalem, sneeringly, closing the door behind him.

Mylan did not answer, but he did indicate the empty skull on the table with his eyes.

"Ah, yes," he said. "I forgot all about that. I should have thrown it away. Or made it into a novelty ashtray or something. But one does get attached to one's own head."

He walked right up to Mylan. "And what do you plan to do?"

"I want my master back."

"Why? He was a fool."

"He might have been. But he was my fool... uh, I mean, my friend."

"Oh. Well, I'm sorry to have to break it to you but..." he leaned forward and whispered in Mylan's ear. "He won't be coming back."

Kalem leaned back and raised the staff until the orb was between them. And then he uttered one word. "Umthatatto."

It was a magical word, of course. No other kind of word would have that many consonants. Anyhow, the moment he said it, Mylan turned to dust.

Now, make no mistake, Rhyfeth is a villain. He doesn't see himself as one, of course. These kinds of villains never do. Truth be told, Rhyfeth was never really the villainous type. He truthfully believed that magic should remain in the world, the problem was, he started to think that he should be the only one to use it. And after being a single, lonely soul tethered to a slowly decomposing corpse over the long, drawn-out centuries... you start to get bitter. Malicious. Vindictive. And you have a long, long time to plan.

And just maybe, go a little insane.

It was the more insane side of his personality that wanted to walk over to the neat little pile of dust that was Mylan and draw a face in it. But he decided against it. For the moment.

Now, he had other things to think about. Mylan had discovered the truth. How long would it be until some of the others would as well? They had accepted him as Kalem so far, but when they started asking questions about Mylan's whereabouts... what could he say? What excuse could he use? A long weekend away probably wouldn't cut it. He looked into the orb, seeing the reflection of another person's face looking back at him. But he was there. Behind the eyes.

He smiled. He didn't need these people. He didn't need anybody. Not now.

Maybe he would draw a face in the dust after all.

As he was just finishing the smile, Rhyfeth decided exactly what he was going to do, and he was going to do it now. No waiting. The very idea made him joyful. He danced through the castle, we can only assume with the Ethera equivalent of 'Tiptoe through the Tulips' going through his head, carrying the orb like a demented Willy Wonka, using the magic to freeze every member of Nightstone that he came to. The last thing he needed or wanted was anyone getting in his way.

Eventually, he made his way to the dungeons. The guard outside Evelynn's cell had barely greeted his master before he became a guardsicle.

Evelynn was watching through the cell bars. When Kalem stepped up to the cell door, she took a step back.

"Don't worry, girl. That..." he pointed to the statue, "...is not your fate."

She edged closer to her uncle. "Why have you done this?"

He didn't answer, only smiled. She looked at his face, drunk it all in. Seeing herself in his eyes. Then seeing the truth.

"You are not my uncle."

The smile on Kalem's face widened. "You are a perceptive one."

Lots and lots of little puzzle pieces fell into place in her head. Her uncle possessed, the orb, the magic... "Are you Rhyfeth or Hydeen?"

This time his eyes widened as well as his smile, like a piece of elastic that was about to snap. "So, you know your history too. If that is the case, then you also know what comes next."

"You want to return magic to the world."

"I do. By any means necessary."

"But why does that mean killing?" pleaded Evelynn.

"Because for a world to be truly at peace, everyone must be of one mind. Better for all to start as we mean to go on."

"That's insane."

The skin suit of Kalem shrugged and smiled. There was some part of him that knew the girl was right. All of those years alone in the tower, rotting, insane thoughts multiplied like flies in his head.

He had had flies in his head at one point. A whole families worth. He'd named them all Franklin.

"I came to tell you, that it will start with Thayorn. I will raise an army of the dead, a whole army of unstoppable warriors and send them there to wipe it out. I just wanted you to know. I'll come back down and tell you all about it."

Kalem gave her a little wave as he walked away. "I am Rhyfeth, by the way. The handsome one."

He walked off, whistling, leaving Evelynn gripping the bars, pulling at them with all her might, begging them to suddenly dissolve away, but they didn't. They remained firm, locking her in with thoughts of death and destruction, and with worry for her parents and all the people she knew.

15

The Kingdom of Thayorn

In his dusty chambers, Rhowern was pulling at piles of books and scrolls, searching for the architectural plans of Nightstone castle that he knew where hidden in there somewhere. As every second passed without the scroll appearing in his hand, his heart began to pound faster and faster.

It had to be there. He said it was there. The whole plan DEPENDED on it being there.

The floor around his feet was starting to fill up with bits of paper as he allowed once precious historical artefacts to fall to the floor. "Where the hell is it... dammit!"

Suddenly, his hand fell upon something that sparked a memory. A large, flat leather wallet, there to protect the documents within. A spark of hope ran through his whole body as he pulled it out. He opened it slowly, hardly daring to look. With all the things he had collected over the years, it could just as well be an old take away menu, never mind the Nightstone plans. Looking down at the papers, he let out a huge sigh of relief as he saw an image of Nightstone looking back at him.

"Oh, thank the Great One."

"Hello? Rhowern?"

Rhowern looked over to the door and saw Queen Jocelyn there. Her eyes were red from crying, and she barely registered the mess all over the floor.

"My lady!" Rhowern scrambled over to her, almost slipping on the greasy scraps of paper. "I found the plans."

"Oh, that's good news."

"This is not really a sensible question, but I must ask, how are you?"

She sighed. "My stomach is churning. I am swaying between sadness and anger. I cannot comprehend, still, what has happened."

"The craving for power makes people do strange things, my lady. And Kalem has always been jealous of his brother."

"But to go so far. Kidnapping his own niece and... and bringing back the magic. How does he know that he can control it?"

Rhowern decided to reveal a little something that had been niggling at him. Something that he had not even told Rolannd, as yet.

"I have been meaning to say, when we were down in the vault and they transported themselves away, I heard the spell being spoken but..."

"But?"

"I did not see anyone speak the word. Kalem, nor his two companions."

"But how did...?"

Rhowern shook his head. "I do not know. That is why I have not said anything. The vault was dark, the fire of the torches was creating shadows all about... maybe I made a mistake. Maybe my eyes did not see."

"So, if *he* did not say the word..."

"Then someone or something else did. Which means Kalem is not alone. Which begs many questions.

Questions that need immediate answers. Answers which I cannot yet provide. But I will try. Until then..."

He held up the Nightstone plans. "We have these."

...

Hargan had been left to his own devices since Evelynn's kidnapping. He heard all about it from those attending to him and mulled over his own options while picking his teeth with a sheep's leg bone. After a while, he came to his own decision about what to do.

...

Rolannd was sat in his bed chamber, perched on the end of the bed, deflated like an old beach ball. He heard what sounded like a flag flapping in the breeze, followed by a scraping sound outside of the bedroom window. Looking up, he almost squealed when he saw a large, lizard-like eye looking in at him.

"APOLOGIES," said Hargan. "I DID NOT MEAN TO STARTLE YOU."

Rolannd walked haltingly over to the window and out onto the balcony. He looked down, seeing Hargan's body coiled like a giant snake around the central spire of the castle.

"I apologise for not seeing you sooner, mighty Hargan,"

"IT IS NOT FOR YOU TO BE SORRY."

"You are welcome to return to Flame Peak. I did not mean to keep you waiting here." Rolannd rested his hands on the balcony rail.

"I HAVE COME TO OFFER YOU MY SERVICES, KING. IF YOU SHOULD NEED TO GO TO WAR, I SHALL BE AT YOUR SIDE."

Rolannd looked up into the great animal's eyes, seeing a deep pool of sincerity there. "I cannot ask that. Kalem has magic. The power to destroy. You would be putting yourself in great danger."

"ON FLAME PEAK I AM ALONE. AND HAVE BEEN FOR SO MANY YEARS. IF I FALL, AT LEAST THEN I WILL JOIN MY BROTHERS AND SISTERS IN THE GREAT BEYOND."

Rolannd was quite emotional at the best of times. When Evelynn uttered her first word - and it was Papa, he cried for an hour until Jocelyn told him to 'snap out of it, you pratt.' So, when Hargan offered his life, he felt the tears welling in his eyes.

The words caught in his throat as he held back a sob. "If it comes to war, I will be most honoured to have you fighting for us. For my daughter."

The tears began to flow freely now.

Hargan saw the wet trails on Rolannd's face. He decided to leave before things got mushy.

"I WOULD APPRECIATE A COW, IF POSSIBLE. THE SHEEP'S WOOL IS CATCHING IN MY THROAT."

"I will have one brought to you."

Pushing his gigantic form away from the tower, Hargan flew back to his paddock-like area that had been prepared for him, curling up like a cat and closing his eyes while he waited for his live beef delivery.

16

Nightstone

Kalem stood on the very top of Nightstone castle, perched like a crow on top of the tallest tower. He had with him, as always, the orb and staff, clasped tightly in his right hand. It was midnight, and a full moon shone brilliantly, it's white light reflecting off the black stone. The spirit of Rhyfeth, encased within that body, rejoiced. The time had come at last. The time for magic to return to Ethera, and to make clear that it was him, and him alone, that would be wielding it.

He looked at the orb. It was moon-like itself, bright and shining. With a violent stab, Kalem thrust the staff into the black stone. The staff and orb stood unaided, like a sentinel.

He placed his hands upon the magical object, and started to recite over and over...

"Retur Marw, retur marw..."

He began by whispering the words, as if he was not allowed to say them. Then gradually, with each repeating, he got louder and louder. Flashes of light began to spit from the orb, striking the stone all around. The air began to sizzle, becoming alive. Above, thunder rumbled. And then, with Kalem shouting the words into the night, a great shockwave of magical power spread outward from the staff, all over Nightstone, and the surrounding grounds. It spread yet further, and further still, creeping like lava.

Then silence.

Kalem waited.

It began slowly. Almost imperceptibly. And then it grew. A scuffling, scraping sound, like fingernails clawing at dirt.

Which is exactly what it was.

Finally, the call of the spell was answered, and the long, forgotten dead of battles past began to crawl from their graves, armour rusted, swords and axes chipped and broken, shields split and rotting. Kalem looked down from the tower, watching the dead answer his call. He could see tens... no! hundreds of them, shambling forward, bones cracking and clicking in the silence of the night. There would be thousands of them soon.

Here was his army. An unstoppable force, that would never tire or sleep.

Took them a bloody long time to arrive though. He had to go and make himself a cup of tea.

When the army of the dead had all gathered, they looked up to him with expectant, grinning faces and hollow eyes. Just as he had looked only a short time ago.

"To Thayorn!" he exclaimed. "And do not rest until it is but rubble beneath your feet!"

As one, they turned toward Thayorn and began their rambling march. Being dead, or dead-ish, they had no real need of paths or roads, and so just took the most straightforward route.

Right through the Darkwood.

17

Edge of the Darkwood

Dawn was approaching when Doran Millar and his six companions trotted up to the edge of the Darkwood.

Well, they didn't trot. Their horses did.

The seven of them looked up at the gnarled trees and dark shadows within, pierced here and there by the morning light.

Doran wondered, as he always did, how the hell he had gotten himself into yet another dangerous situation. Seemed to be fate.

Time to own it.

Captain Greeve had chosen him and the others for their skill and dedication (so he had said), provided them with swords, daggers, and swift horses and with only one objective. Return the princess, no matter what.

To be fair, Greeve himself had apologised that their course would take them through the Darkwood, but stealth – and speed - was of vital importance.

"How many trolls do you think are in there?" Said Lidon, one of the other men, his sword already drawn.

"Probably hundreds," someone answered.

"Or thousands," said another.

Doran turned to face them. "Enough, now." he said authoritatively. "We've been given an important task, and we must do it. A princess needs rescuing, and we've been the ones who have been given the job."

He looked at their faces. Some of them he knew well- Lidon, Fusco, Tripper, Samson, two he knew only in passing. They were Freel and Gorman. He saw in their faces the same look he no doubt had on his – apprehension and fear. But Doran had decided it was time to face those feelings head on. The princess had done no harm to anyone, and despite a still aching arse from travelling on the back of a dragon, he had decided he was going to do his absolute best to get her back.

"It's all very well being told we're the best people for the job," whined Fusco, but they're not the ones flinging their nuts on the anvil and hoping the blacksmith is going to miss."

"This is for the princess," said Doran. "She's done no harm to anybody. And what about you, Lidon, and you... Freel, isn't it? Don't you have children?"

Both men nodded.

"And I'm sure you wouldn't want your children to go through anything like this."

"To be honest," said Freel, "given the way our boy acts sometimes, I think I'd rather be the one who was kidnapped."

That provoked some welcome, if subdued, laughter.

The ice that was the mission, seemed to thaw a little.

"Alright then," exclaimed Doran, "Let's go and get her back. Now remember, trolls attack from above, so they'll be hidden in the trees. They hate clambering around on the floor, so don't bother looking down. And it's dawn. Sunlight is really painful for them, so hopefully that will keep them away. But it's not called the Darkwood for nothing. The sooner we get in, the sooner we get out again."

Taking a deep breath, and with a sound of sliding metal as each drew their swords, they entered the Darkwood.

18

They were immediately met with a musty, heavy wall of uncomfortably warm air, that made beads of sweat break out on their brows. Shafts of angular sunlight streaked through the dimness. They could hear small woodland creatures, chittering as if they were in a very bad mood indeed, and then scurrying off into the undergrowth.

The ground was mossy and covered with dead leaves and twigs. It undulated like rumpled carpet because of the massive tree roots that burrowed underground, so big now they threatened to pierce the dirt floor.

Each of the men scanned ahead and above, looking and listening for any signs of movement.

So far, nothing.

None of them dared speak, in case they would disturb something dark and brooding within the forest. Doran pointed the way, and they all followed him, travelling single file, the gaps between the trees not offering any more space than that.

The men could see hints of vaguely unpleasant things hidden within the folds of the dark. Bones picked clean – animal or human, it was hard to tell. Cobwebs, hanging like fine lace, with the drained bodies of flies, mice and small birds hanging limply from them.

Not exactly a summer holiday destination.

If all goes well, thought Doran, *we'll be through here in a couple of hours.*

And that's when things went to hell. Just goes to show, thinking isn't always good for you.

Tripper was last in line.

He had been dutifully scanning trees above for any threat. Movement to his left caught his eye. Tensing, he squinted, trying to get a better look. Suddenly, a squirrel, scrawny and bad tempered jumped from one tree to another, squealing miserably at it passed.

Tripper smiled nervously.

At that moment, a large, hairy body dropped heavily on him from above. He screamed as the troll's dirt encrusted talons dug into his shoulders. As blood began to spurt from the wounds, Samson and Freel wheeled around as best they could in the cramped space and went to help.

The troll grunted and snorted, before burying its head into Tripper's neck, the tusk like lower teeth burrowing into the skin. Blood spurted all over the place like an erupting geyser.

Samson got there first, stabbing the troll viciously in the back. It squealed, loosening its grip and turning toward its attacker. Preparing to jump onto Samson, Tripper used the last of his ebbing strength to stab the troll in the throat, killing it instantly, the body sliding down off the horse and landing with a thud on the floor.

They all looked at Tripper, sad and astonished. He looked down at himself, covered in blood, his breath slowing, the light in his eyes dimming.

"Bastard." he said, before falling to the ground, dead.

Before anyone could say anything at all, the horses began to neigh and moan, becoming restless.

Then the forest came alive.

Shadows detached from the trees, large and dangerous. With big bloody teeth.

"Attack!" shouted Doran. "Move through them if you can!"

They turned back to the way they needed to go, swinging their swords wildly, hacking at anything that moved. Occasionally, they heard squeals of pain, which told them at least some of their sword strokes had found their mark.

Despite all their efforts, it was hard to pick up speed, encumbered as they were by long, hairy arms and sharp claws and teeth.

Suddenly, a human scream rang out. Doran looked toward the noise, seeing Fusco pressing his hand at the wound in his arm. Blood poured out between his fingers. Angered and in pain, Fusco turned the offending troll into a shish kebab. Doran looked at the others – flailing wildly with their swords, more trolls crawling down the tree-trunks toward them.

This mission is going to end before it's even properly began, thought Doran.

A troll appeared directly in his eyeline, roaring into his face. Drool dangled like string from its mouth. It darted for him, and Doran held up his sword horizontally in front of his face. The troll's mouth closed around it, the sharp edges of the sword biting deep into its gums. The troll's eyes widened, like every family member at Christmas when they realise, they've bitten into chocolate covered coconut.

The troll detached itself from the blade and jumped back to the nearest tree, blood dripping from its face.

It eyed him venomously.

There were yet more gathering in the trees. Doran even thought he could see a few angry grey squirrels in amongst them all, eager to join the massacre.

His heart sank.

"We cannot get through this!" shouted Lidon, piteously, his head bleeding from a nasty cut.

Hope ebbed away.

Then the atmosphere changed.

An ominous feeling, like the air before a storm. Trolls started to squeal like frightened pigs. They grabbed hold of the surrounding trees and started to pull themselves up and out of harm's way.

"What the hell is going on?" shouted Gorman.

They didn't have to wait long for an answer.

Moving through the trees like wraiths, the dead army of Kalem/Rhyfeth marched through the Darkwood, on their single-minded quest to get to Thayorn. Doran's eyes widened in amazement. In fact, all of the men's jaws dropped.

"I... uh... don't know what to say." spluttered Freel.

Some of the trolls, curious and hungry, came back down from the trees and attempted to attack the zombie soldiers. As soon as anything attempted to deviate them from their mission, the dead turned viciously on their attackers, tearing them apart like paper.

Some of the trolls' hefty bulk managed to unbalance the zombies and send them tumbling backward onto the floor. Even then, as the creatures tried to bite and rip at their victims, the dead simply stood back up, striking and killing the trolls who had taken them down.

It was then the trolls decided they had had enough.

They left them to it, hurling themselves back up to the safety of the tree canopy, nursing their injuries and their malice, and rueing the fact that none of them managed to get a decent meal.

Amazingly, the army did not attempt to hurt or kill Doran or any of his men.

He saw Lidon attempt to strike one with his sword, and immediately called out for him to stop.

"No!" he shouted. "I don't think they'll do anything to you if you don't do anything to them."

Lidon lowered his sword.

Doran was proved right. The soldiers kept moving.

Gorman shook his head in disbelief. "This seems a bit extreme, even for Kalem."

"We have to warn Thayorn," said Samson.

Doran looked at Fusco, the pain from his shoulder injury etched upon his face.

"Fusco, I want you to ride back to Thayorn as fast as you can. It doesn't look like these things have much in the way of speed."

As he was speaking, the dead carried on walking past like an endless river.

"Warn them," he continued. "Now go!"

Fusco didn't need telling twice.

Looking back at Samson, Lidon, Gorman and Freel with his best hopeful expression, Doran ordered them onwards through the Darkwood and then onto Nightstone. The trolls would not bother them anymore.

...

As soon as Fusco burst free from the Darkwood, he raced back toward Thayorn, hardly giving his horse time to breath in the fresh air. He still grasped his wounded shoulder, grimacing in pain as the blood began to dry against his skin. He could see Thayorn in the distance. The Darkwood was so near, the great kingdom never really disappeared from sight.

Now, he just wanted it to get closer, as quickly as possible.

He looked back at the Darkwood, already growing smaller behind him. He could just make out the figures of the dead appearing out of the trees like walking nightmares. He had no idea what anyone in Thayorn would be able to do against these monsters, apart from praying.

Maybe, he thought, *praying was all anyone had left.*

19

Nightstone

Kalem had been down in the kitchen, making himself a snack. At first, he considered unfreezing the cook but then he remembered he could just 'magic' something scrumptious together from the food available.

Not the most dignified use of magic, but hey, who was going to stop him.

He ended up with a mutton sandwich and mug of ale.

After stuffing his face, he decided to go back upstairs for what he called 'the main event.'

Giggling maniacally to himself on his way out of the kitchen, he headed toward the great hall.

When he got there, he pointed the orb toward the fireplace and uttered a spell, immediately igniting a fire there.

In the corner of the room was a guard. Frozen to the spot, with a look of confusion on his face. Kalem wandered over to him and reversed the spell. The guard, naturally, was confused and shaken, completely unaware of what was happening.

"My... my lord. I had the strangest dream..."

"Yes, yes," said Kalem, barely listening.

He led the confused guard near to the top table, where he would usually sit during feasting. Manoeuvring his little meat puppet to exactly where he wanted him to be, he suddenly held the staff and orb out in front of him.

"Hold that," he said.

The guard didn't think it was a good idea to refuse, plus, he didn't know what the hell was going on anyway. He took hold of the staff.

Kalem made little micro-adjustments to the guard and how he wanted him to hold the staff. Ramrod straight.

When he was happy, he said "Rhetheen," which froze the guard again.

Still giggling, he sat himself at the head of the table, the orb three feet away at eye level, perfect for viewing the coming destruction of Thayorn.

"Show me," he said to the orb, in a very commanding voice.

The silvery, smoky interior of the orb suddenly became clear, and the Kingdom of Thayorn was shown there. *Ready and waiting,* he thought, *for the end to arrive.*

He was a little perturbed, however, to see crowds of people streaming into the large gate set in the castle walls. The gate that was specially designed to ward of oncoming attacks. He saw farmers and peasants, arms around their families, scurrying into the safety of Thayorn's walls.

Kalem looked into the orb, quizzically.

"But how could they know?" he said aloud.

His ghoulish soldiers had definitely not made it all the way there yet. They were too slow for that, marching ceaselessly on their old, and probably arthritic bones.

"Probably a scout," he mumbled to himself. "Or a farmer out chasing a sheep. Must have spotted them coming."

He gave no thought to any other possibility.

"Doesn't matter," he said confidently. "A big gate won't stop them. And it won't stop me."

20

The Kingdom of Thayorn

King Rolannd wasted no time at all preparing for the attack when Fusco rode back in through the gate, bleeding, exhausted and pale as milk. In the past, if he, or anyone else, had said anything about a skeleton zombie army on the march they would have been called a piss-artist and had a bucket of water thrown over them.

But not now.

He immediately ordered the army to be put ready, and every subject of the kingdom not already inside to be brought into safety.

Hargan smiled inwardly. *A fight at last,* thought the dragon. *Finally, something worth waking up for.*

...

The Ffhugees were once again of two minds. Or three. Or four. So, what exactly was The Great One playing at now? He wants the magic back but he's sending it to kill us? Or do we have to kill it, to prove that we are the rightful heirs to Ethera? Yes, maybe that's it.

Or maybe it isn't.

It was at this point, a great number of Ffhugees made their way to The Wizard's Tipple to get drunk. Given the state of things, alcohol had a very good chance of making everything seem clearer.

...

Perched atop the castle tower with a telescope, Rhowern scanned the horizon. In the distance was the Darkwood, a fitting backdrop for the horrific sight in front of it.

The army of the dead filled the landscape. Rhowern watched them come, their slow, inevitable march making him shiver.

It wouldn't be long now.

...

Nightstone

Doran and the others spilled out of the Darkwood, bruised and bleeding, but all things considered, in pretty good shape. They gave their horses some time to settle, the animals being so much more sensitive to the... 'weirdness' of everything around them. Thankfully, the dead were far behind them now. And ahead, about half hours ride away, was Nightstone.

Beckoning them on, they rode steadily toward the black, rather boxy looking structure.

As they rode, Doran pulled out the leather wallet which contained the architects plans for Nightstone. Getting nearer, they slowed to a trot, and he opened it up.

What they were aiming for was a small ravine, somewhere to the left of the castle, maybe two hundred yards away. He studied the plans then looked ahead, searching for any sign of it in front of him. Spotting the ravine, he used hand signals to direct the rest of them toward it.

They slowed right down now, entering the ravine as quietly as possible. Trying to be inconspicuous on a horse isn't the easiest thing in the world to do, but dammit, they tried their best. They kept their eyes and ears open, in case of any guards.

So far nothing.

Moving further on through the ravine, they could hear the unmistakable sound of trickling water.

Looking down, a very, very thin stream of the life-giving liquid flowed beneath them. They kept going.

Finally, they came to what they were looking for. A vent. A kind of sewer pipe, about five feet high. Bars were fixed upon it, but they had rusted away at the base over time, making entrance to the castle relatively easy.

Doran dismounted, and the others followed suit.

There were some straggly old trees dotted about, secure enough to tether the horses.

It was the work of minutes to bend and detach a couple of bars, giving them enough space to enter. They would all have to duck to walk through the pipe, but that wasn't the problem. Accidentally stabbing each-other up the arse however, was. They decided to keep their swords in their scabbards for now.

Ripping a rotten branch from a nearby tree, Doran fashioned a flaming torch to guide them on their way.

"Come on then," he said. "Let's go."

21

The sewer pipe had an unpleasant smell that drifted lazily into their nostrils, making their noses twitch.

They all unconsciously sped up, trying to find the end of the tunnel as quickly as possible. Their footsteps made light, tinkling splashing sounds as they stumbled quickly through the water.

Lidon's back was starting to ache from bending down for so long in the low tunnel. He kept his complaining to himself, not wanting to add any more misery to the already miserable situation.

"This tunnel is getting on my nipple ends," said Gorman, gruffly.

"Agreed," said Doran.

"Same here," added Lidon, relieved.

"Hold up!" hissed Doran. "I can see an opening ahead."

They approached carefully and quietly, expecting at any moment the silhouette of a guard or servant to pass by the circle of light – the literal 'end of the tunnel.'

Nothing.

They moved all the way forward. Before pressing himself up to the bars to look out, Doran extinguished the torch in the water.

When he looked, he saw that the sewer entrance was at the end of a kind of slope – like guttering. The light was coming from above. It was the sky.

"I think we're in a small courtyard. Looks like all the runoff from the weather must come down here, and the sewer pipe carries it out."

"What about the bars?" asked Samson. "Are they rusty here, too?"

Doran looked down. The bars were indeed rusty and crumbling. Easy to break. He told them so.

"What about guards?" said Freel.

"Can't really tell from this angle. We'll have to get out of here first."

After a few swift boots to the metal bars, combined with strategic swearing, two came loose. Doran held one in his hand while the other threatened to clatter loudly to the ground. Thankfully, Lidon caught it before it could announce their presence.

The guttering was smooth and slippery. They each used their daggers to stab viciously into the brickwork, giving them some much needed leverage. After much shoving and pulling, the four of them were stood in the courtyard, panting heavily after the effort.

Still, no guards.

Seeing a doorway, they headed stealthily toward it.

Preparing for anything, Doran whispered a countdown. "3...2...1."

They swung the door open and came face to face with a shocked looking guard. Freel prepared to strike when Doran suddenly stopped him.

"Wait! Look..."

With the rush of adrenaline subsiding, the men took a long look at the guard in front of them. Either he was playing musical statues, or he had nerves of steel. Doran reached out and gave the guard a little shove.

The figure rocked lightly back and forth.

"He's... he's frozen," said Samson. "Like a statue."

"How?" asked Gorman.

Doran shrugged his shoulders. "I have no idea. But I doubt it's anything good."

"If everyone else is like this then we won't have much of a problem," said Freel, cheerfully.

Doran wasn't entirely convinced that things were going to be so easy. "Come on. Let's find the princess."

22

The Kingdom of Thayorn

The dead had arrived.

On the vast green plain that lay in front of the main gate, the zombie soldiers gathered. Already they clawed at the thick, wooden doorway, as if slowly scraping away at it would finally gain them entry.

Inside, the army, led by Captain Greeve, formed ranks, spears, swords and shields at the ready.

"Stay ready!" Called the captain. "They can do nothing until they are through that door."

Each soldier felt a pang of positivity. The main gate was thick oak, reinforced with steel. It would take hours, maybe days for any army to penetrate. It was the fact that every enemy on the other side of the door wasn't breathing that continued the sense of unease.

The king watched from the main tower, Jocelyn by his side, shaken by the unbelievability of it all.

"Do you think our daughter is still alive, Rolannd?" asked the queen, tears welling in her eyes.

"She is," he answered with confidence. "Because I can't believe anything else."

She rested her head on his shoulder.

"Besides," he said, "we have something Kalem doesn't."

...

More and more dead poured themselves toward the door like a river against rock, hammering against the wood. It was the weight that started the door buckling. Just slightly. A centimetre at most. But the movement was noticeable.

It was then they erupted in flame.

Above, Hargan flew by, smoke pouring from his mouth after the first burst of fire. Below, the dead soldiers continued hammering against the door, despite the fact they were on fire. Hargan, happily humming to himself, wheeled around for another attack. Coming lower this time, he roared again, an inferno spewing from his huge mouth.

Now, the soldiers below began to disintegrate, the heat from the flames turning them into dust.
Seeing the dragon flying by, letting loose a curtain of destruction, made the soldiers of Thayorn cheer.

Even Captain Greeve smiled. "They are not getting in here."

...

In Nightstone, Kalem was rather unhappy. He had forgotten about the dragon.

He had forgotten about the *bloody dragon.*

The temper tantrum that had threatened to erupt began to subside.

"It's okay," he said to himself. "They ain't seen nothing yet."

Placing a hand on the orb, he closed his eyes and began to mutter some dark, dangerous words. The orb glowed, lighting up the entire hall. Kalem opened his eyes, the spell finished. He took his hand off the orb and the glow diminished.

...

All the way over in Thayorn, a spear of light flew through the sky. It hissed like a comet and headed directly for the main gate.

The flash was blinding.

Every soldier of Thayorn covered their eyes in pain. A split second later, there was a deafening explosion and the gate ceased to exist, sending soldiers from both sides flying backwards from the shockwave.

There was a ringing in everyone's ears.

Captain Greeve had landed on his front, covered in dirt and splinters. His body ached as he turned himself over, looking directly at the huge hole where the protective gate used to be.

There was nothing there now. Apart from the steady flow of skeleton soldiers which started to march through.

...

In the Wizard's Tipple, the landlord had already locked himself in the cellar. He had tried, unsuccessfully, to wake up the still drunk Ffhugees who had passed out on the tavern floor, their robes spread around them like spatters of red paint. Ever since they had discovered the wonders of alcohol, every member of the Ffhugees who had visited The Wizard's Tipple had decided it was probably the best place to be.

When the gate erupted, the High Priest, Kevin, finally stirred. His eyes creaked open, letting in the daylight. His brain immediately told him that was a bad idea, and that he should close them again.

Which he did.

Some of the other Ffhugees started to move as well, the mother of all hangovers welcoming them into her embrace.

Kevin opened his eyes again, his brain still arguing with him all the way. But he had to open them. SOMETHING was going on, and he needed to know what it was.

Outside they heard an unmistakeable sound. The sound of fighting. They could hear swords clashing against swords, shouting, screaming, wailing. The sounds of pain and anguish.

Kevi... no, the High Priest, decided they had to help.

Rallying the rest of the woozy clerics, he decided it was time to do something. Time to help those who needed it most. Time to minister to the injured and the dying.

Bracing themselves, they opened the door of The Wizard's Tipple and stepped out, seeing a scene of carnage and horror the likes of which they had only heard of. Blood, death and... skeletons? LIVING skeletons?

The High Priest of the Ffhugees blinked once.

"Sod that," he said, and closed the door.

23

Nightstone

Doran and the others continued to explore the lower levels of Nightstone, careful to be as quiet as possible. They had come across a few more frozen people, most of them with either shocked or completely bewildered looks on their faces.

They also saw some rats scurrying through the hallways, which went to prove, at least, it wasn't the entire castle that was frozen. Just the people. Doran started to worry about Evelynn. If she were frozen, he wouldn't have a clue how to fix it. And he very much doubted that Kalem would be willing to help.

"Hold up!" said Lidon, suddenly. He pointed to the left. A doorway, half hidden by shadows. It was easy to miss. "Let's look through there."

They headed toward the door, stopping only for a moment to have a listen.

Nothing.

"Come on," said Doran, opening the door.

It was the dungeons.

A single guard stood frozen to the spot.

"Is anyone there?" came a voice.

It was Evelynn. She had heard the squeak of the door hinges. Pushing her face to the bars, she called out. "I'm here!"

They rushed down to her cell, clattering like a brass band.

"Thank The Great One," exclaimed Doran. "We were starting to panic. All these frozen people about the place. I'm guessing it's Kalem's doing."

"Not quite," answered Evelynn.

Before he could query her response, Samson produced the keys from the frozen jailer's belt. In a swift click of the lock, the door was opened, and Evelynn was free.

"Thank you for coming for me," she said. "But we can't go yet. My uncle Kalem... he's been possessed or something. Taken over by the spirit of Rhyfeth."

Their eyes widened.

"Rhyfeth?" said Gorman. "How?"

"I don't know. But he said he was sending an army of the dead to attack Thayorn. He wants to kill everyone who doesn't believe in the magic."

"Yeah, we... uh, met some of them," mumbled Lidon. "Not the most talkative of chaps."

"How are we going to stop him?" pleaded Freel. "He's a wizard!"

"I don't know that either," admitted Evelynn. "But if we don't do it, who will?"

Doran knew she was right. *So here we go again,* he thought. *Another dangerous mission. Another chance to die. Horribly. Time to decide.* He took a deep breath before exclaiming...

"Let's get the bugger!"

...

In the main hall, Kalem continued to watch Hargan rain fire down upon his army. For those that were only singed, it was nothing. A minor inconvenience at most. For those directly in the path of the fiery inferno... well, let's put it this way, dust can't walk.

He was getting annoyed. So annoyed, his left eye began to twitch. It was such a large, consistent twitch, it felt like someone was playing a drumbeat on his face.

Finally, he decided it was time to even the odds.

Placing his hands on the orb again, he closed his eyes and muttered "dyad draigg…"

A thin mist emanated from the orb, curling around him and then rising up toward the ceiling. The mist was indistinct at first, but as it rose, it began to take shape.

And to grow bigger.

The shape was lithe and lizard-like. Hazy scales began to form as skin for the still growing emanation. Then wings began to sprout from its back.

And still it grew. Bigger, and bigger.

And bigger.

Eventually, the shape dissolved through the ceiling, re-appearing upon the very roof of Nightstone. The shape was clear now, more defined.

It was a dragon. As large as Hargan, misty grey with eyes glowing the fiercest red. It roared long and loud, a malicious, frightening utterance.

Far down below, Evelynn and the others heard it, each one too scared to even utter a question of what had made that sound.

Above, the dragon took off, flying toward battle.

And victory.

24

The Kingdom of Thayorn

The tide of the battle turned constantly.

While the dead could not, technically, be killed by sword or axe, cut them down enough and they became but a collection of small, wriggly body parts.

And of course, Hargan's fire was doing a spectacularly good job of exterminating the zombies still outside the city gates.

But the dead did not tire, and humans did. The repeated effort of fighting off the endlessly unstoppable force was beginning to show on the soldiers faces.

Captain Greeve was not sure what to do. He had no reserves. This was it.

"Come on, men!" he shouted. "Force them back!" He grabbed one of the men to his right and pulled him close.

"Find the city carpenters and blacksmiths. If we can push them back, we need to find a way to block the gate. Go!"

The scared soldier went immediately to his task, rushing into the heart of the city as fast as weary legs could carry him.

Greeve refused to give up hope. As long as he breathed, as long as he could fight, he would never stop.

The roar made everyone look up. Even the dead showed a little interest.

It wasn't Hargan. It sounded different. Sharper. Crueller.

Hargan turned in mid-air, looking toward the sound.

He saw, as they all did, the spectral dragon, its eyes blazing, heading straight for them.

Before he could engage, the enemy dragon spewed a torrent of green flame, hitting Hargan full on. He wheeled round, sending his own fireball back at it. The fireball spread like a blanket over the grey beast, making parts of it dissolve, but quick as a flash, the animal regenerated and swooped in for another attack.

The sky became alive with orange and green fireworks, the sound like thunder. On any other day, it would look like a celebration, but today, it was a prelude to doom.

With no Hargan to fend off the dead, the ghouls began to pour freely into Thayorn. Hope began to fade and every soldier still breathing started to falter. In a last-ditch attempt to rally his troops, Greeve ran forward, screaming angrily, striking left and right with his sword, hacking mercilessly at every vacant, bony face. As he sliced the head off one, he did not see another approaching from behind, plunging its sword into the valiant captain's back.

The once determined light left Greeve's eyes, and he crumpled lifelessly to the ground.

Above, the roaring continued. The two magnificent creatures clawing and swiping at each other, Hargan becoming bloodied and tired. Every injury he inflicted upon his ghostly foe simply disappeared, as if it had never been. Green and orange flame enveloped them both, as they corkscrewed around in the air, creating a tornado of fire.

Hargan knew he couldn't possibly win.

He didn't mind.

Die doing what you love, he thought. *Ain't that the dream?*

25

Nightstone

They could hear the whooping and cheering through the old wooden door. Evelynn approached it stealthily, preparing to open it, just a crack.

Doran tried to stop her, doing his best to indicate that a) it was dangerous and b) he was technically in charge.

She gave him a look that suggested a) she knew it was dangerous, and b) she was the princess, so there.

Truthfully, he didn't have a comeback.

She opened the door, and the sounds of exultation grew louder.

...

Kalem smiled and cheered as he watched the great dragon, Hargan, fall out of the sky and crash helplessly onto the ground. Sure, his body crushed a lot of the rambling ghoul soldiers, but he didn't care.

The dragon was dead. Thayorn's only feasible and effective defence gone, just like that.

There really was no stopping him now.

He was so distracted by happiness, he failed to notice the shadows creeping in. Evelynn, Doran, Lidon, Samson, Freel and Gorman, lurking in the darkness beneath the ridiculous tapestries.

Evelynn spied the orb and staff, set, as it was, in the frozen hands of a Nightstone guard. That was the key. The thingy that would get them out of this mess somehow. They had to get Kalem, or Rhyfeth, or whoever, away from that orb. And, if possible, they had to get Kalem back. If he still had a sense of awareness in that body, wherever he was, surely, he could see all this had gone too far?

Evelynn and Doran looked at each-other. They had discussed on the way a kind of/sort of plan. Distraction. The more he was distracted, the better chance there was of whisking the orb away. Through hand-signals, Lidon, Freel and Samson began to creep slowly around to Kalem's left, while Evelynn, Doran and Gorman went right.

They moved as slowly and carefully as they could. Every now and then, Evelynn looked over at Kalem's face, illuminated by the light from the orb.

He looked truly manic.

She knew she needed him to remove his focus away from what he was doing and direct it completely toward her. Her breathing quickened. She couldn't believe, only a short while ago, she was panicking over the First Rule Day ceremony. And now, here she was, about to face a ghostly wizard who had taken over the body of her uncle and was waging a magical war with an army of dead soldiers.

Not your average day.

She stood up.

Doran panicked, trying to pull her down again, but she batted his hand away.

"Kalem!" she called. "Or Rhyfeth. Whatever you want to be called."

The wizard was so confused for a second, he had to spin completely around, eyeing the corners of the room.

Then he saw her. Standing about twenty feet away from him, in the centre of the room.

"And how did you get out, my little troublemaker?" he said, slimily. "You're obviously smarter than I gave you credit for. Tell me, would you like to see the destruction of your kingdom?" He beckoned her over. "Come and see. It's nearly over."

"I just don't understand the reasoning, here," she said. "Why not just... ask? You've assumed everyone in Thayorn is against the return of magic, but you've never really found out for sure."

He took a couple of steps toward her, leaving the orb unguarded.

"I know," he replied. "But you see, the thing is, it's complicated. I was stuck, tethered to my own rotting corpse for hundreds of years. Betrayed by my own kind. Betrayed by humanity. What's wrong with a little vengeance? A little shock and awe? Okay, it might seem rather extreme and even petty, but look at your uncle."

He took another step toward Evelynn.

"So jealous was he of your father and everything he had, he came into the Forbidden Lands, looking for a way to bring him down and take the kingdom for his own. All because he didn't want to be second best. *Now that's petty.*"

As he was monologuing, Lidon crept out of the shadows and moved toward the orb. Evelynn saw him but did her best not to give it away.

"So," she said, "because of all that built up rage and resentment, you are willing to destroy thousands of lives?" She shook her head, sadly. "You ever thought of seeing a counsellor? Or having a lavender bath?"

Kalem smirked.

"I like you, human. Maybe you can be my pet. You amuse me."

"I don't think you'll find this next thing funny."

He cocked his head like a dog, unsure of her meaning.

Lidon grabbed the staff and orb, but the effort of pulling it out of the frozen grip of the guard made the stiff body topple over.

Kalem spun round and immediately sent a bolt of lightning from his fingertips that hit the unfortunate guard and made him explode like confetti.

As Lidon ran with the orb, lightning bolts followed close behind, sparks falling around him like rain. They were so close he could feel his butt hair curling. While he was distracted, Gorman ran toward the wizard, his sword drawn, ready to strike. But Kalem was too quick. He turned toward Gorman and shot a lightning bolt from the hip, as if he were some Wild West gunfighter. Gorman was too close for the bolt to hit, but the force of the lightning threw him off his feet.

Doran and the others all rose from their hiding places, running in a myriad of different directions. Kalem became disorientated, firing aimless shots in all directions. In the chaos, he spied Lidon, running toward the doorway that led back into the hall.

Kalem screamed in anger.

The other warriors ran toward the insane sorcerer, preparing to strike. Distracted by his need for the orb, he sent a shockwave of energy behind him, sending Doran, Evelynn and the others flying back across the floor.

Lidon was almost at the door when he suddenly felt a force like a magnet pulling at his back. Lidon fell forward, trying to grip at the floor with his one free hand.

Kalem stalked over to Lidon. "Good try, insects. But not good enough."

He bent down to pick up the staff, his fingers curling around it. Suddenly, Freel jumped onto his back, sliding his arm around Kalem's throat. Gasping for air, he released his grip on the staff and tried to pry himself free.

Doran ran up to the wizard and stabbed him in the side.

Kalem screamed, and so did Evelynn. As bad as things were, she didn't want her uncle to die.

He faltered and fell to his knees, Freel releasing his grip.

Evelynn ran to him, looking into his face. His eyes. Kalem looked up at her, his expression changing, as if there were a fight going on beneath his skin. His eyes brightened and dulled.

The princess looked at him with hope. "Uncle Kalem. Uncle... is that you? Are you in there?"

The voice that came out of his mouth was halted and broken.

"Evelynn... he... help me..."

He reached out, grabbing her shoulder and pulling himself up. Blood poured from the wound in his side.

She helped him to his feet. "How do we set you free?"

Kalem placed his head next to hers; his lips close to her ear. "I am free."

Smiling, he drew a small dagger and held it to Evelynn's throat, grasping the top of her body with his left arm.

"The thing is, little niece, Rhyfeth has given me everything I need. Why would I want anything else?"

Lidon got to his feet, holding the staff, the orb on top still showing visions of Thayorn under attack – the sphere filled with death, destruction and fire. Kalem looked into his eyes, his pupils narrow and focused. "Give us the orb, or she dies."

Us, he had said, thought Evelynn. *They were partners now. Kalem and Rhyfeth.*

"Don't!" She shouted.

"Give it to him," said Doran. "We were ordered to take her back alive. That's all that matters."

Lidon looked down at the staff, then back up at Evelynn, with a dagger at her throat. Reluctantly, he held the orb out to Kalem. He loosened his grip on the princess and held out his hand to take the staff.

The point of the blade came away from her throat.

Evelynn and Doran locked eyes. "Duck!" He shouted.

She fell to her knees and Samson rushed up from behind. He had been creeping up toward the wizard all this time, as Kalem had issued his threats and ultimatums. Doran had been watching him. He stabbed the wizard in the back, while Evelynn took hold of the staff and lifted it above her head, hurling it down toward the floor with every ounce of strength she had.

It would have looked very impressive in slow motion.

The orb and the staff came apart, the sphere rolling away from its holder. Kalem looked up vindictively at the people surrounding him. His eyes met each of them in turn, landing finally on Evelynn.

"It's not over yet."

Kalem closed his eyes and started to whisper "Enad E Frwd, enad e frwd..."

Evelynn gasped like she had been dunked in cold water. A ghostly image of the princess began to rip itself away from her body, tearing like a piece of paper. She started to scream. Doran ran forward, stabbing Kalem through the chest. The words of the spell faded away like a shadow in sunlight.

Rhyfeth now had no soul to anchor to. It howled like a dying animal as it left Kalem's body. With nowhere to go, Rhyfeth dissolved like smoke. Despite everything, Evelynn knelt down next to her uncle's body. He was gone. Truly gone.

She didn't feel anger, only sadness, and a deep need to go home as soon as she could. Looking around at her rescuers, she smiled, with tears flowing from her eyes.

"Thank you," she said. "Thank you all."

...

In Thayorn, the grey dragon was hurtling like a meteor toward the ground, spewing green fire. Soldiers ran in all directions, like ants. Suddenly, the dragon began to fade, become transparent, then disappear altogether, the flames along with it. The army of the dead fell to the floor, truly lifeless.

There was silence. The soldiers of Thayorn stopped in their tracks, looking about them, taking in the sudden silence. A sense of disbelief, followed by a murmur. Low at first but growing like the roar of a waterfall, it became a cheer that rang out across the entire kingdom.

In the tower, Jocelyn looked at her husband.

"How?"

Rolannd smiled. "I don't know," he said. "But I think it means our daughter is coming home."

EPILOGUE

Mordath Harbour

The dark green sails of the royal flagship caught the breeze and pulled the great vessel forward, cutting like a blade through the sapphire blue water. A burnished gold dragon decorated the sail, and it fluttered and undulated as if alive and waking to the morning of the world. A fitting tribute to the great Hargan.

Evelynn stood at the bow, looking out at the ocean before her. In the distance, she could see the land beyond, veiled by a silver mist.

But that was not their destination.

Above the shouts of the sailors and the general activities of ship-board life, Evelynn heard footsteps approaching behind her. She turned to see her mother, Queen Jocelyn, resplendent as usual, even as the boat tossed about on the ocean. Behind her was Rhowern, humming merrily and eating a chicken leg.

"Hello, mother," she said. "Is father still... indisposed?"

Before Jocelyn could answer, a retching, bellowing sound came from somewhere aft.

"Bleeeeeeuuuuuurrrrrghhhhh!!!!!!!"

With the slightest of blinks, and maybe a minor twitch of her nose, the Queen answered. "Yes."

"I never realised sea-travel took so much out of him," said Evelynn.

"He was never one for it. Much preferred to stay on dryland. Feet firmly on the floor" answered the queen.

...

The previous morning, they had awoken early. The people of Thayorn were barely stirring themselves when Rolannd, Jocelyn, Rhowern, Evelynn and the Kings-guard trotted out of the main gates on their fine horses. They were heading for Mordath Harbour but were in no great hurry to get there. This was to be a solemn journey, a journey for the family to look over the Land of Ailani, its green plains, tall mountains, and glistening lakes. To think about the cost of winning the great battle, the losses, and the gains. Doran Millar was amongst them. As were Fusco, Samson, Lidon, Freel and Gorman. All official members of Princess Evelynn's personal guard now, thanks to their amazing service. Doran himself had been made Captain of the entire Thayorn army, taking the place of the heroic Captain Greeve.

They looked very splendid indeed in the brand-new armour. Very spiffy. And they were enjoying all the attention they were getting from the ladies of the kingdom, now that they were wearing it.

The Ffhugees watched them go. Dressed once again in their red robes and orange hats, they said a blessing to The Great One and asked that their journey be safe and without incident. They knew, of course, what the big plan was, and as with Hargan, they were of mixed feelings on the subject. So, after their blessing, they returned to The Wizard's Tipple. Alcohol, they had decided, was the ultimate key to opening their closed minds, and letting them really get to grips with all the contradictions and inconsistencies of the Ffhugee religion. It really got you to the core of it.

Either that, or you got too drunk to care.

As they had journeyed on, Evelynn looked to her left, seeing the shadowy trees and dim green canopy of the Darkwood. Even in the peaceful morning, crows wheeled and circled above the trees. To her right, the waiting sea, with its rolling waves glinting like diamonds in the sunlight. A month had passed since the great battle. It had been a month of rebuilding. And a month of mourning, too. After all, it was Rolannd's brother – her own uncle, who had died, along with Greeve, Tripper and many brave Thayorn soldiers.

The cawing of the crows became the screeching of seagulls as Mordath Harbour approached. The harbour tower rose above the surrounding town, and a sonorous bell began to ring to announce the approach of the arriving royals. It had been a long time since Evelynn had seen Mordath. She had been only a very small child on her previous visit, but even so she remembered the salty smell of the harbour and the ocean beyond.

Evening was falling like a shadow upon the day when they arrived. The flagship was moored and ready for the following morning.

That night, they slept in the town's finest inn, each of them with a guard outside their door. Evelynn had a package with her, wrapped in the smoothest silk. All night long, she held it close, holding it to her like a precious toy, an endless stream of thoughts passing through her mind.

In two days', her re-scheduled First Rule Day ceremony was going to take place. Any doubts or fears she once had had gone now. She just hoped this time the whole thing would go without a hitch. No spectral dragons, no zombie soldiers and no insane relatives.

…

As Evelynn and her mother stood together on the deck, Evelynn still holding the parcel in her arms, Rolannd walked unsteadily up to them.

"How are you, father?" asked Evelynn, a slight smile playing on her lips.

"Absolutely fine," he lied. "How much longer are we sailing for?"

"I thought another hour. Just to get far enough away from land."

"An hour?" exclaimed the king. He began to turn green. Trying not to attract too much attention, he sidled over to the port side of the ship, leaning over the rail.

"I'm sure he'll be alright," said Jocelyn.

"Bbbbllllleeeeeuuuurrrrrrgggghhhh!"

"I'm sure he will be," replied Evelynn.

Despite Rolannd's frequent trips to the rail, Rhowern continued to eat his chicken leg and hum cheerily. The nonsensical music he produced accompanied the kings retching like some kind of symphony. Or opera. 'Don Vomittini.'

"Do you think he really will be all right, though?" asked Evelynn, concern in her voice. "I mean, it was Uncle Kalem who tried to take over the world and kill a lot of people. Even though he was possessed for some of it."

"Your father mulled this all over for a long time, Evelynn. But I think he has made peace with it now."

"What's all this?" asked the king, wiping his face with a damp towel.

The queen turned toward her husband. "We were just talking about Kalem."

The king nodded. "Ah, yes. Kalem. Stupid bugger."

They sailed on until they were many miles from shore and the sun was high.

"I think we have come far enough; don't you reckon?" Rolannd asked, hopefully.

Evelynn nodded. "Yes."

She lifted up the silken parcel and unwrapped it, revealing the orb.

Magic, as discussed, can be contained but not destroyed. They held the staff back in the castle vault. The orb, however, was the much more dangerous part. This time, rather than keeping it, they decided to get rid of it altogether. A heavy wooden chest, weighed down by heavy stones, had been prepared. It was opened now, and the orb placed into it. The chest was then closed, locked, and wrapped with a heavy iron chain.

It took Doran and two strong sailors to lift it over the side and drop it in with a thunderous splash. They all stood looking over the rail, watching the chest sink to the depths.

Rhowern dropped his chicken leg.

It had been a most difficult decision, letting the orb go. Magic had created this world, was part of the very fabric of it, but as the recent events had shown, there would always be those who coveted it for their own and wanted to use it for their own selfish reasons. Humanity it seemed, could not be trusted. And so, for that reason, it was decided...

Magic was to end today.

At least, the sorcery kind. For Evelynn, Jocelyn and Rolannd, family was magic. Life was. Love was. Letting the orb go was a farewell to spells, mysticism, and darkness.

A farewell to magic.

THE END

AFTERWORD

Fantasy is no easy thing to write. In fact, I'm still not 100% sure I did get it right. I tried my best, I'll say that.

The key to writing fantasy, I think, is verisimilitude. That is, it needs to have a sense of realism and believability within the world in which it is set. Most fantasy is quite serious and solemn and, when done right, can be completely transformative – able to take you away to magical lands filled with dragons and wizards, and sweep you off into some wild adventure.

And you believe it.

Even though it's probably filled with lots of outlandish places and silly names.

I tried. I really did. I wanted my fantasy to be

serious. I must have tried two or three times, but it was all just a little bit too po-faced for my liking, and I felt it could do with nothing better than a few jokes and silly asides. Indeed, as soon as I started to put them in, it all came together. It clicked. And I still think it has verisimilitude, even with fart jokes.

There is funny fantasy out there. The undoubted king of which must be Terry Pratchett. His novels not only have incredible detail, well-rounded characters and deep-rooted lore, they are also extremely hilarious and even moving. My work is but a pale imitation, but at the very least I had a go.

And I enjoyed every silly moment of it.

D Woods

July 2024

ABOUT THE AUTHOR

As a playwright, Damian has written more than fourteen plays and sketches, all of them available on www.lazybeescripts.co.uk. He has since written a number of books for children, including The Cowardly Knight, Wicked Ways and A Little Nonsense. And for mature readers, Dracula Reborn, Dracula's Legacy, Now and Forever and Split Second. All of these are available on Amazon.

Printed in Great Britain
by Amazon

af8e73b9-f606-41ad-b482-6b9c015edaa3R01